Wholehearted

By the Author

In Too Deep

Deeper

Wild Abandon

Hearts Aflame

Flesh and Bone

The Seeker

Chasing Love

Conquest

Wholehearted

Praise for *In Too Deep*

"Ronica Black's debut novel *In Too Deep* has everything from non-stop action and intriguing well-developed characters to steamy erotic love scenes. From the opening scenes where Black plunges the reader headfirst into the story to the explosive unexpected ending, *In Too Deep* has what it takes to rise to the top. Black has a winner with *In Too Deep*, one that will keep the reader turning the pages until the very last one."—*Independent Gay Writer*

"…an exciting, page turning read, full of mystery, sex, and suspense."—*MegaScene*

"…a challenging murder mystery—sections of this mixed-genre novel are hot, hot, hot. Black juggles the assorted elements of her first book with assured pacing and estimable panache."—*Q Syndicate*

"Black's characterization is skillful, and the sexual chemistry surrounding the three major characters is palpable and definitely hot-hot-hot…if you're looking for a solid read with ample amounts of eroticism and a red herring or two you're sure to find *In Too Deep* a satisfying read."—*L Word Literature*

What Reviewers Say About Ronica Black

Wild Abandon

"Black is a master at teasing the reader with her use of domination and desire. Black's first novel, *In Too Deep*, was a finalist for a 2005 Lammy…With *Wild Abandon*, the author continues her winning ways, writing like a seasoned pro. This is one romance I will not soon forget."—*Just About Write*

"The sophomore novel by Ronica Black (*In Too Deep*) is hot, hot, hot."—*Books to Watch Out For*

"If you enjoy complex characters and passionate sex scenes, you'll love *Wild Abandon*."—*MegaScene*

Hearts Aflame

"Sleek storytelling and terrific characters are the backbone of Ronica Black's third and best novel, *Hearts Aflame*. Prepare to hop on for an emotional ride with this thrilling story of love in the outback… Wonderful storytelling and rich characterization make this a high recommendation."—*Lambda Book Report*

Deeper

"This sequel to Ronica Black's debut novel, *In Too Deep*, is an electrifying thriller. The author's development as a fine storyteller shines with this tightly written story.…[The mystery] keeps the story charged—never unraveling or leading us to a predictable conclusion. More than once I gasped in surprise at the dark and twisted paths this book took."—Curve Magazine

Flesh and Bone

"Ronica Black handles a traditional range of lesbian fantasies with gusto and sincerity. The reader wants to know these women as well as they come to know each other. When Black's characters ignore their realistic fears to follow their passion, this reader admires their chutzpah and cheers them on…These stories make good bedtime reading, and could lead to sweet dreams. Read them and see." —*Erotica Revealed*

The Seeker

"Ronica Black's books just keep getting stronger and stronger… This is such a tightly written plot-driven novel that readers will find themselves glued to the pages and ignoring phone calls. *The Seeker* is a great read, with an exciting plot, great characters, and great sex."—*Just About Write*

Chasing Love

"Ronica Black's writing is fluid, and lots of dialogue makes this a fast read. If you like steamy erotica with intense sexual situations, you'll like *Chasing Love*."—*Queer Magazine Online*

Wholehearted

by

Ronica Black

2012

WHOLEHEARTED

ISBN 13: 978-1-60282-594-9

This Trade Paperback Original Is Published By
Bold Strokes Books, Inc.
P.O. Box 249
Valley Falls, NY 12185

First Edition: February 2012

Credits
Editors: Cindy Cresap and Stacia Seaman
Production Design: Stacia Seaman
Cover Design by Sheri (graphicartist2020@hotmail.com)

Acknowledgments

Thank you, Bold Strokes Books, as always, for supporting me and taking this book on. A big thank you to my editors Cindy and Stacia. And to all those at BSB behind the scenes, much love and gratitude to you all, always.

For Cait

CHAPTER ONE

The juvenile justice courtroom was small, windowless, and strangely stifling for such an early morning hearing. It felt as though a hundred bodies had already been gathered and then herded through, depriving the room of much-needed oxygen. The gray carpet seemed to shadow this feeling with its well-worn dinginess, made more apparent by the harsh fluorescent bulbs. One blinked and buzzed in the front corner. Attorney Grace Hollings didn't know whether to squint or to widen her eyes to try to focus better. Instead, she glanced to her right and squeezed her nephew Jake's hand as they sat at the defendant's table. To her dismay, he pulled away and turned to stare at the wall. For a second it looked as though he could see through it.

"Are we ready to proceed?" the judge asked from her elevated bench.

"We are, Judge," the assistant district attorney answered from the next table.

Grace studied the petition under her palm. Her nephew, Jake Hollings, was charged with theft and resisting arrest. This didn't include his priors back in Ohio, which were numerous, though not violent, and mostly consisted of truancy. She fought a sigh and listened as Judge Newsom, who happened to be a friend, spoke to her.

"Ms. Hollings?" Judge Nancy Newsom's voice betrayed nothing, certainly no recognition of the fact that they knew each other.

"Your honor, I call Jake Hollings."

"Jake?" Judge Newsom said. "Please have a seat up here."

Jake walked with his shoulders slumped to the witness chair. He seemed so small in his oversized navy dress slacks and men's oxford shirt. The sleeves of his shirt were folded back into thick rolls, causing his arms to look gangly. But he'd insisted on a men's size, refusing a boy's, which would have fit him better. That was the way it was with Jake. His way or the highway. And he'd told her countless times that he had no problem hitting the highway himself if he didn't get his way.

As he sat, he gave Grace that familiar pinched look, as if he were annoyed or in pain. With or without it, he looked so much like a cross between her and his mother Gabrielle, it sometimes took her breath away. With his blond hair, fair skin, and light brown eyes, he could've easily passed for her son and often people assumed he was, which irritated him no end. He would always insist, "I have a mother, I don't need another one." As if he'd said the words again, he continued to glare at her, fanning his long lashes at her as he waited. He was so very handsome but so very wounded.

"Jake, I need you to answer my questions loudly and clearly, okay?"

He shifted as if still trying to be Joe Cool, too good for any of this.

"Okay."

At least he answered. Thank God juvenile court was less formal compared to adult court.

"Did you skip school on March seventh of this year?"

"Yeah."

"To date, do you know how many days of school you've missed since starting at Rio Grande?"

"I didn't, but they said it's like twenty." He motioned toward the district attorney's table.

"Twenty-two," Grace clarified.

"Yeah."

"Why don't you like school?"

He shrugged. "I do. I just—I get bored. And somebody always has something better to do, you know?"

"Jake, did you and your friends go to the Pizza Shack at approximately eleven a.m. on March seventh of this year?"

"After we took off from school, yeah."

"Did you eat at the Pizza Shack?"

"Yeah. I had two slices and a Coke."

"Did you pay for your food or drink?"

He shifted again as if uncomfortable in his chair. "No."

"Why not?"

"Harrison paid. Then Frankie and I ate off his plate."

"And this was a buffet your friend Harrison paid for?"

"Yeah."

"So Harrison paid for one buffet and one drink, and you and your other friend Frankie used his plate and drink cup to eat and drink for free?"

"Yeah."

"Was this the first time you had done this at the Pizza Shack?" This wasn't going to be easy, but they had to do it. For his sake.

"No."

"How many times had you stolen food and drink like this from them?"

He sighed, obviously not liking the question or the answer he was about to give. "Two times before this." He hadn't liked the word *steal*, but she'd discussed it with him and made him see how it was indeed stealing. Even if Harrison paid for one. He'd reluctantly agreed and apologized.

"When the manager called the police on March seventh, what did you do when you saw the police pull up at the Pizza Shack?"

He shifted and turned red. "We took off."

"What specifically did *you* do?"

"I ran out the side door and down the alley."

"Did the officer tell you to stop?"

"Yeah. He yelled and cursed and stuff. Said stop."

"But you kept running?"

"Yeah."

"Why?"

Again the pinched look came. "Because it was the cops, Aunt Grace. I didn't want to get in trouble."

"Were you afraid?"

He shifted some more and stared beyond her and she knew she'd lost him. "Jake? Were you afraid?"

Come on, Jake. Just admit it. Admit the fear. It's okay.

"I was afraid of getting in trouble."

She resisted a sigh, knowing he would fight her on this.

"When the officer tackled you, what did you do?"

"I—he arrested me."

"Did you fight him?"

"No."

"You went limp, correct?"

"I—"

"Jake?"

"I didn't fight, okay?"

"Why not?"

"Because—because it was stupid. He was heavy."

She wanted to close her eyes. Jake was even too afraid to admit he was afraid. He just couldn't let his guard down, not even when his freedom was on the line. The truth was he had been afraid, and he had gone limp as soon as the cop had touched him. She moved on, hoping he would at least admit to what was next.

"Jake, are you sorry for what you did at the Pizza Shack? Are you sorry you stole?"

"Yeah. I mean, I didn't really think about it at first. Harrison paid, you know? But yeah, it was wrong. I can see that now. And—I'm sorry."

Grace looked to Judge Newsom, who had been watching them both closely with her dreadlocks swept back in a ponytail and reading glasses on the tip of her nose. Grace hoped like heck she'd give her and Jake a break on this.

"Your honor, Jake has admitted to the charges and has expressed his sorrow for committing them. He also has paid the Pizza Shack for the March seventh incident and the two times before. The money was taken from his own allowance."

The judge nodded and looked to the assistant district attorney. "Anything further?"

"Yes, your honor, if I may?"

"You may."

Grace sat and chewed her lower lip nervously as the opposing attorney, Ally Murphy, began. Like Judge Newsom, Grace also knew Ally. But their relationship had been more than friendly colleagues. They'd only seen each other twice and it had been two years ago, but the memory of their encounter was still as fresh as a morning rose, causing Grace to shift uncomfortably in her chair. Ally showed no discomfort, however, which was to be expected, considering her job. She'd only given Grace a polite nod when they'd entered the courtroom. One which Grace had returned and then fought a blush. Why did Ally have to be assigned this case?

"Jake, you said you were sorry for stealing from the Pizza Shack?"

"Yeah."

"But you stole from them three times."

He sighed. "Yeah."

"You also missed twenty-two days of school and you ran from the police. Is this correct?"

He looked to Grace, who nodded, encouraging him to tell the truth.

"Yeah."

"So really, it's just like you said, Jake. You're just sorry you got in trouble. Sorry you got caught."

"No—I…"

"Nothing further."

"Your honor, may I re-approach?"

"You may."

She was hoping it wouldn't come to this, but she had no other choice if she wanted to keep Jake out of juvenile detention.

"Jake, is it true you've only been here in Phoenix for six months?"

"Yeah."

"And you were in Ohio before this, correct?"

"Yeah."

"Where your mother lives?"

"Yes."

"Where is your mother today, Jake? Why isn't she here?" Her voice cracked as she mentioned Gabrielle, her younger sister.

"She's—in rehab."

"She's been in rehab a lot, hasn't she? For drugs?"

He swallowed. "Yeah."

"And when she hasn't been in rehab, she's been on the streets, or at whereabouts unknown, right? Leaving you alone for days at a time?" It was difficult for her to get the words out. She'd only recently found out how bad things had been. Gabby had always been good at putting on a show when she visited. And their mother, who was better at sweeping things under the rug than Gabby, had always made sure to keep the house afloat with rent and food. But the rest had been left to a young boy. A young boy all alone.

He swallowed and nodded, looking away.

"Your mother's been addicted to heroin for many years, hasn't she, Jake?"

His voice was soft. "For as long as I can remember."

Dear God, had it been that long? How could she have missed it? How could her mother have ignored it?

"But you're here now. With me. Your aunt. Hopefully, we can change things, right?"

He nodded. "Yeah."

"Please tell the court why you don't like school, Jake. The other reasons."

"Do I have to?"

She nodded and moved forward. "Jake, have you been attacked at school?"

"Aunt Grace," he said.

"Jake, please. Just answer yes or no."

"Yes."

"Back in Ohio? You were physically beaten?"

"Yeah."

"And after that you haven't liked going to school, have you?"

"No."

Judge Newsom cleared her throat. She'd obviously heard enough. "Please be seated."

Jake followed Grace to their table and buried his head in his hands. He often tried to hide his emotions, but when they did come out they took forms of what she saw now. His body shook and he began to sweat. She touched his shoulder, but he flinched and wouldn't look up. If things continued like this, he would most likely bolt from the room and curl up in a ball to cry.

Judge Newsom spoke. "Ms. Hollings, I trust you read the psychological examination?"

"I did, your honor."

"Based on this and what I've heard here today, I would have to suggest that Jake enter therapy and attend a supervised rehabilitation facility."

Jake shook harder.

No. Please, no.

"I've also taken into consideration his previous truancy and curfew charges in Ohio. Just prior to you getting him, Ms. Hollings, Jake was taken into the custody of child protective services due to serious neglect at home. Is this correct?"

"It is," Grace replied.

She continued. "However, he admits to these latest charges and, Ms. Hollings, as his guardian, you are willing to take responsibility as well?"

"Yes, your honor. I am and I have. Jake has only been with me for six months and we're still learning each other. But I can assure you he is loved and cared for here."

"Very well, I see no need for this to go to trial. However, I am sentencing Jake Hollings to a ranch for boys for a period of two months. He must complete the program and wear a monitoring bracelet until the program is completed. At such time Jake is to return to school and attend daily. If you fail the program or fail to go to school, Mr. Hollings, you will be placed in juvenile detention. Is this understood?"

Grace placed a hand on his back and he jerked.

"You have to answer her."

"Yes," he muttered through his fingers.

Grace felt like crying. A ranch for boys? He was being taken away from her?

"Very well. Jake will attend the Healing Soul Ranch daily for two months. He will return home with you nightly, Ms. Hollings. And afterward he will go to school and return right home for a period of six months. After which he can attend school and do as he and you please."

Grace too placed her face in her hands as court was adjourned, but she did it out of relief. He could come home! It was done. It was over. This case had worried her well beyond any other she'd ever faced. Jake. He was going to be okay. She stood, gathered her things, and as Jake stood, she hugged him. He wasn't being locked up!

"It's over," she said as he stiffened beneath her. "We can go on now."

"Wrong," he said, his eyes distant and cold. "I have to go to some ranch." But his shaking had stopped and some color had returned to his face. At least he wasn't going to collapse on her or run away and curl into a ball. She touched his face, trying to get him to focus, but his cool brown eyes avoided hers.

She led him out of the courtroom and noted that, as usual, he never seemed to be happy. She'd noticed it a week after he'd arrived. Nothing made him smile. Not even when he did well on his video games. He would just shout "Yes!" but there would be no grin or anything more said. He also didn't like to be touched. But she kept trying, knowing he needed love and affection.

"Ms. Hollings?"

Grace turned in the main lobby area to find a bailiff heading toward her. "Ms. Murphy would like to see you."

"Oh."

"I'll keep an eye on Jake." He nodded toward him and Jake sighed and shuffled to a nearby chair. Around them, other juveniles waited with loved ones for their hearings. She felt for them, knowing what that wait was like. She also wondered what Ally wanted. Grace followed the bailiff's instructions and wound her way down the hall to an empty meeting room where she knocked and entered.

"Grace Hollings," Ally said, rising from behind a round table. Her smile was broad and bright and she was just as beautiful as ever with tanned skin, flashing dark eyes, and long midnight hair. Her lavender blouse seemed to caress her skin just right, and Grace at once smelled her lotion as she approached. Ally gave Grace a lingering, breathy kiss near her ear.

"Still as beautiful as ever," she said, pulling away slightly.

"So are you," Grace said.

"So why didn't we continue seeing each other?" She held Grace's elbows, her eyes dancing with intensity.

"I don't know. I think we're just too much…"

"Alike?"

Grace smiled. "Something like that."

"But I enjoyed our time together."

"I did too."

"We should do it again sometime."

Grace nodded but she doubted she would. She had Jake to worry about. Despite that, though, she didn't turn away when Ally leaned in and kissed her softly on the lips. It stirred her with its softness and warmth and for a second, she longed for more.

"I have to go," she finally whispered as she pulled away.

"I know." Ally blinked and her lips shimmered with gloss and traces of Grace. "I just wanted to say hello and to wish you luck with your nephew."

"Thanks. I think I'll need it."

Ally laughed softly. "You'll do fine. The place he's going to will be good for him. It will help."

"I hope so."

"Call me sometime and we'll have dinner."

Grace nodded.

"Or call me if you have any more problems. I know some really good people who can help with Jake."

"Okay."

"Or call…" She kissed her again. Long and soft, causing Grace's knees to weaken. "If you should need anything for you."

Grace struggled to gather the breath to speak. "Will do."

"Good." She backed away and squeezed her hands. "Good-bye, Grace."

Grace gave a half smile and opened the door. "Good-bye."

She walked briskly down the hall, touching her lips delicately and pressing them together to cover any trace of Ally's gloss. The taste of her lingered and she found she quite liked it. It had been a long time since she'd been kissed, and she mused another one would be a long time coming as well. She repressed a small grin and focused on Jake.

He was slumped in the chair as she turned the corner. The bailiff stood and Grace gently shook Jake's shoulder. He jumped up and followed her quickly out to the car as if he couldn't get out of the place fast enough.

"What was that all about? Is she going to come after me again?" he rattled off. The sun was fierce and bright, and Grace fumbled in her purse for her sunglasses. She slid them on and opened the door to her black Mercedes sedan.

"No, she just wanted to make sure I knew I could ask her for help if needed."

"Like for what?" He closed his door, popped an earbud into his ear, and powered up his iPod.

"Like for you." *And me.*

"I don't need any more damn help," Jake said, leaning back and closing his eyes. She could hear his music playing through his earbuds.

"We all need help, Jake." She glanced at him and then at the open road. "We all do."

CHAPTER TWO

There you go, there you go," Madison Clark called out and then whistled to the young gelding as she tugged on the rope and led him around the pen. "Good boy. Good boy." The gelding, Guinness, had a prosthetic lower hind leg but was progressing really well considering. She couldn't be prouder, and the smile burning her cheeks felt good. "That's a boy."

The day was warm bordering on hot in the low nineties with the sun low and a nice breeze stirring the nearby trees. Healing Soul Ranch was eerily quiet, and she was very much enjoying her Sunday with her horses and dogs. Lila, one of her border collie mixes, was trotting alongside Guinness. They'd become fast friends and Lila, in all her white coat glory, justified herself as the herder of the ranch. She, along with her sisters Beamer and Flaca, pretty much ran the property alongside Madison. They knew the routine, the commands, and what was to be expected. Flaca, all legs and feistiness, raised her head as Madison whistled again. Madison gave her five more minutes before she was either following Lila and Guinness or out searching for lizards scurrying through the wildflowers.

"He's looking good, Maddy," said Marv, her friend and ranch hand for years, as he approached.

"I was wondering if I'd see you today."

"Miss me?"

"Like the summer heat."

He gave a gruff laugh. "I figured."

Madison focused on the horse. "Yeah, he's doing really well.

Look at him go." She quickened the pace and the gelding responded eagerly, trotting in a large circle around her. Lila ran to the side of the pen and panted, intent on watching and giving him plenty of room.

"His frame is good, muscles taut. And look at that coat. Shining like the sun itself," Marv said as he stroked the end curls of his mustache. "And the way he handles those boys with a saddle, I'd say he's ready."

"Me too." She smiled and slowed his pace and after a few more minutes, she brought him in close. With her hand under his muzzle, she kissed his nose and spoke. "Good boy, Guinness, good boy. Are you ready for a new home, boy? A forever home? Maybe with two kids, a big ranch, and two loving mommies?" He snorted and bobbed his head. She laughed. "I thought so." To Marv she said, "Guess I'll be giving the Kramers a call tonight." The Kramers had been sponsoring him and had already put down a payment to adopt him. They were just waiting for her to give them the green light. And Guinness was now a definite green light. "It's good news," she said, shielding her eyes. It was always their goal to adopt out their horses to forever homes. They came in battered and broken and she and Healing Soul sent them out healed and loved. It was how things worked, and business had been fulfilling, to say the least.

"That's great news," Marv said, looking as he always did in dark denim Levi's, leather cowboy boots, and a white T-shirt. When he worked he usually wore a long-sleeved button-up shirt to protect his arms from the sun, but in his off time he preferred the James Dean white tee. His wide-brimmed straw cowboy hat did the same as his long-sleeved shirts, protecting his handsome face from the rays of the sun. She thought he looked a lot like Sam Elliott, with gray hair, gray scruff, and a curly gray mustache. His grin was wide and sincere and many a woman had considered him well beyond handsome. But Marv was married to the cowboy way, and there didn't seem to be anyone out there in the world who could slow him down or change that. Not even her and her constant bickering that he find someone. "We'll have to take more photos of him for the website. Along with his new family."

"It will be interesting to see his before and after," Madison said, stroking him down.

"Yes, it will. That poor boy came in here looking like death himself."

She nodded and kissed Guinness again, replacing his fly mask after doing so. The nylon netting covered his eyes and protected him and all her horses from flies; they also helped to protect them from the harsh rays of the sun.

"Why don't you go home, Marv? It's Sunday. I know I'm pretty, but I'm not that pretty." She sometimes felt bad with him always being there. He was too good a man to spend Sundays working with her.

He chuckled. "You are that pretty, darlin', but I'm here for that colt."

"Right." She laughed. He just couldn't resist a new horse on arrival day. The big tough guy was a softie underneath and she mused that his heart was made of leather, just as tough and durable as the rest of him, yet soft and pliable when it needed to be. He was an asset to her healing ranch, one she could never replace. His stern but soothing ways worked miracles on her horses and even more so on the kids. She held up her hand and he tossed her a brush to use on Guinness. "He'll be here any minute."

"What do you know?"

"Well, it's not good."

Marv sauntered inside the pen, curry comb in hand, and took to grooming Guinness from his other side.

"The owners took off on the colt shortly after the dam died. Just left him there to die right next to his mother." She hated the mere thought of it. Poor little foal.

"Sweet Jesus."

"Yep. So he was malnourished and neglected, to say the least."

He breathed, long and slow. "Well, it's not the worst we've had."

"No, it's not."

"So he's okay now?"

"Beverly gave him colostrum and an IV and all that. She's got him on a bottle, but he still needs some serious TLC."

"You gonna put him in with a mare?"

"I was thinking about Mazey."

He grinned. "Mazey's my girl."

"I know. I knew you'd be pleased."

"I think she'll do great."

"Let's hope the colt takes to her." They finished brushing Guinness and led him to the stables. The flagstone path they followed was even and smooth, framed with wildflowers and trees. Palo verdes, mesquites, and mastics threw much-needed shade over the path and between the pens. The oaks and cottonwoods were closer to the house, towering high above it. She'd invested thousands in trees when she'd acquired the three hundred acres seven years earlier. The shade and beauty they provided was priceless and she knew the horses appreciated it as well; the summer sun was brutal.

She slipped on her shades and stared into a similar sun as noise came from up the drive. "Looks like he's here."

A muddy dually truck was pulling a trailer and kicking up dust as it drove carefully toward the ranch. Madison handed Guinness to Marv and waved as her longtime friend Beverly finally brought the growling truck to a stop.

"Ranch looks great!" she said, bounding out.

"Thanks." It had been a few months since she'd last seen Beverly, and she'd been a little thankful for it, knowing that no horses had needed homes from her rescue until recently. No news was good news when it came to Beverly.

"It just looks better and better. And so do you. Just get better with age. Like those wines you collect." Beverly's blue eyes danced and the freckles across her nose and cheeks seemed to as well.

"Are you saying I've aged?"

Beverly hopped into her for a hug. "With that short dirty blond hair and those hazel blue eyes, you'll be a heartbreaker forever. You'll never age."

"Ha!"

"You're supposed to say, 'Well, neither will you, Bev.'"

"Neither will you, Bev."

"Shut up."

Madison laughed. "How have you been?"

"Oh you know, can't complain. The rescue's doing well and Bryce is keeping me busy."

"Still trying for a baby?"

"Yeah." She smacked Madison's arm playfully. "Devil."

"That's not what I meant."

"Sure."

"It'll happen."

"I hope."

Sadness overcame Beverly and her posture fell a bit. But just as quickly she took a deep breath and straightened.

"Come on. Show me my new boy," Madison said with a small smile.

Beverly unlocked the back of the trailer. With grace and care, she carried the baby colt out and placed him on his feet. Madison walked to him and knelt, holding lightly to the rope around his neck. He moved his face away from her and kicked once to get away.

"Well, he's got his feet under him."

"He's feisty. Just your type."

"Thanks."

"You love the feisty ones. Always up for a challenge, that's you, Madness."

"Maybe."

She watched him trot a little and rear his head.

"How is he with humans?"

"Other than me? Not so good yet. He's all legs and pride."

"Yeah, that's just her type, all right," Marv said as he exited the stables to join them.

"Feisty?"

"No. All legs and pride."

"You're both just so funny. Can you see me laughing?" Normally, she didn't like teasing about her nonexistent love life, but with these two she didn't mind. They, along with her best friend Rob, knew her best, and unfortunately, they were mostly right. Mostly.

"You may not be, but we are. Ain't that right, sugar?" He held out a hand to Beverly and gave her a kiss on the cheek as she enveloped him.

"I told her he's feisty, just like she likes."

"I do not like feisty." Feisty women drove her nuts. The stubbornness and nonstop demanding.

"I was talking about the horses, Madness." Beverly smiled and half hugged Marv.

"Uh-huh."

"I wasn't," Marv said, chuckling.

Madison shook her head. "You work for me, old man."

"Don't remind me."

"Can we focus on the colt, please?"

Marv grumbled and came to stand next to her. The baby was walking the pathway, keeping his distance. His rope was long and she wasn't worried about him running off, considering the stable was on one side and they were on the other.

"Looks healthy."

"Yep."

A bee near a bed of wildflowers frightened him and he came tearing back toward them. Madison laughed, excited at his health and playfulness. All things considered, he looked great. Marv seemed to think so too as he knelt and whispered things to him while holding his rope. "You're a handsome fella, ain't ya?" He placed his hands on his withers to still him. "Shh, that's a boy." His hands continued down his flank to his belly and then back up where he looked at his teeth. But the colt jerked and tried to run.

"He bit me," Marv said.

"Yeah, he does that."

"Thought you knew better, Marv?"

"Yeah, yeah." He shook his hand. "Just a nip. He looks good though. Healthy."

"He should," Beverly said. "He had an IV and we gave him enough colostrum to feed an army."

"So he's eating okay?"

She tugged her ball cap tighter. "He did for me, but he didn't for my staff. So he might give you some trouble with the bottle. You might want to hang one or try the bucket."

Marv released him and watched as he trotted away, obviously wanting nothing to do with any of them.

"Feisty," Marv said, straightening. "He's gonna be a stubborn little fella." He looked to Madison. "You want to put him into the stall with Mazey?"

Madison nodded and started to follow him when her cell phone rang. "Marv, go ahead." She retrieved it from her leather belt and flipped it open. "H and S."

"Yes, is this Madison Clark?" The voice was feminine and smooth, but confident with strength. It got Madison's attention right away.

"Yes." She turned away from the stables to lean on Beverly's truck.

"Ms. Clark, my name is Grace Hollings. I wondered if I could talk to you about my nephew, Jake? He's starting there tomorrow."

"Of course. But can I call you back in about an hour?"

"Oh. Well, no, I can't. I need to go into the office. I need to talk to you now."

Madison blinked. This was why she didn't usually answer unrecognized numbers on Sundays. "Can we do it tonight, then?" She really wanted to get the colt settled in.

"No. Look, I just need to ask if Jake can get a ride in and out from the ranch every day."

"Excuse me?"

"Since he's not staying the night, I thought you might have a shuttle or something."

What did she think this was, a hotel? "No, sorry, no shuttle."

"Is there any way he can get a ride with someone else? Maybe someone who lives in our area?"

"Ms. Hollings, is it?"

"Yes."

"Is there going to be a problem getting Jake here every day?"

"Obviously, yes. Which is why I'm calling. Can someone give him a ride?"

"No."

"Why not?"

Was she kidding?

"I can't discuss my other clients and their living arrangements, but I can tell you there is no one."

"Well, how do all these kids get to you every day?"

"If they live at home, the parents."

Madison could tell that stung by the quick intake of breath she heard over the phone.

"You can't bring him in, Ms. Hollings?"

"No, I can't. I'm an attorney and I work close to downtown. I am in court some days, and your ranch is near Tonopah."

"Well, we're right off I-10. Most folks make it to work in plenty of time since the boys need to be here by six forty-five every morning."

"Six forty-five?"

Had she not read over the material?

"Yes, ma'am. Have you not read the brochure or the e-mails I sent out?"

"Of course. I—most of it. Six forty-five is so early."

Madison laughed a little. She'd had uncooperative parents before, but this one, she had a feeling, was going to take the cake. "Yes, it is. We do our best to meet and mingle with the sun around here. Get our days started early."

"I guess so."

There was a long pause, and Madison briefly thought she might have disconnected. She could hear Beverly and Marv talking and laughing and she was missing it. She wanted to see Mazey with the colt. "Is there anything else I can do for you, Ms. Hollings?"

"Ha. Um, no. Thank you, but no." Her sarcasm was oozing through the phone, causing Madison to grimace.

She forced herself to sound positive. "We'll see you tomorrow, then?"

"God willing."

"Good night, then."

Ms. Hollings hung up without a reply.

"Nice lady." She flipped her phone closed and headed inside the stables, still stung from the conversation. Part of the program at the ranch was to instill responsibility and punctuality into the boys. Having them arrive every day at six forty-five was important when it came to instilling these virtues. They needed to know that people counted on them and that these recovering horses depended upon their care. Parents fighting her on it didn't set a good example.

She came up on the stall where Mazey, one of her rehabilitated horses, was trying to nuzzle the new colt. He scurried from her at first but then slowly allowed her to smell him and nudge him around. Beverly was thrilled and Marv was grinning from ear to ear. So far so good, but she was still irritated at Ms. Hollings. So irritated she couldn't let it go. Had she done or said something wrong?

"Let me ask you something, guys," she said. "This is a healing ranch, right? A place where injured and sick horses come to be rehabilitated with the help of young men who need a bit of behavioral rehabilitation themselves, right?"

"Yeah."

"We are not in any way a hotel, are we?"

Marv shook his head. "What now? Another parent wanting to pay you to keep their kid overnight?"

"No. This one wants us to provide a shuttle service."

"Good Lord," Beverly said. "Really? These parents do this kind of thing?"

"Oh, you wouldn't believe it." Madison rested her arms on the door to the stall and lowered her head.

Marv explained. "She had a man try to sell her his son. His son liked it here and he figured Madison could use the permanent help—"

"And he wanted money," Madison finished for him.

"That's terrible."

"It's why these boys are here. A lot of it is poor parenting." Madison reached in and stroked Mazey's delicate flank. Her hide felt rough with small patches of fur and scarred skin. It twitched as Madison scratched it. Mazey snorted and shook her head in approval. She loved to be scratched and stroked, despite the horrors she had lived through.

Madison closed her eyes and breathed in the smells of the stable. Hay, oats, leather, dirt, manure. It all soothed her and grounded her. She thanked the gods for these animals and their healed and gentled souls. These horses had been mistreated, just like most of the boys. What was wrong with people? She asked herself that nearly every day and never found her answers.

"Let it go, Maddy, or you'll go mad," Marv said, relaying one of his favorite lines. He could always tell when she was stewing.

"I don't know how you don't," Beverly said. She half hugged Madison and held her tightly. "I just have to deal with the horses. I couldn't imagine having to worry about kids too. You do good things. Don't ever forget that."

"You too," Madison said, feeling herself closing off well before the tears came and the worry continued. She had to shut off and let it go, like Marv said. Deal with each issue as it arose and then release it. It was the only way to stay sane at Healing Soul Ranch.

"I'd better get going. Bryce is making me Sunday supper."

"Sounds good," Marv said.

"You've got a colt to attend to," Madison said, forcing herself to smile.

"Ah, he'll be fine."

Madison knew he was kidding. She'd be surprised if he didn't spend the night looking after it. She hoped he would. More and more lately she found the loneliness of her large home daunting. It made her feel hollow inside, like something that was impossible to fill despite her trying.

"Right. Let's try that bottle first," she said. "Then we'll have supper."

Madison followed Beverly out to her truck and watched her crawl inside to retrieve all the info she had on the colt. She handed the file over. "You got everything else you need?"

"Sure do. And Rob will come check on him tomorrow." Rob

wasn't only her best friend, he was also a fellow rescuer and vet. When it came to horses, he could almost compete with Marv.

"Call me if you need anything." Beverly wiped away a sudden tear. "I can't hug him good-bye or I'll cry. And to think I only had him for a week."

"I know." Madison patted her shoulder. "Come by next week and see him."

"I might just do that."

"You will."

Beverly smiled. "See ya, Madness."

"See ya."

She waved as she drove away, and Madison watched the dirt snake up behind Beverly's truck as she headed out. The sun seemed to meet her at the end of the road, and Madison crossed back into the stables, hoping to get the colt settled with Mazey before dark. But cursing from Marv greeted her as she came upon the stall.

"Damn stubborn boy," he said, bent over, hand on knee, dripping bottle in the other.

"Won't eat?"

"Won't eat! He won't even stand between my legs."

"Great." She laughed softly. "Guess Beverly wasn't lying." Mazey, however, was very curious about the bottle and she was licking the milk that fell on the hay. "Think you'll have any luck later?" She hadn't seen it firsthand, but the colt was over in the corner flicking his tail and pacing, in no mood for being held still.

"I doubt it. Probably gonna take a few tries."

"Well, come on. I got some pintos on the stove. Your favorite."

He perked up and an eyebrow lifted as he repositioned his hat on his head. "You knew I was coming, didn't ya?"

"I know you like a rattler knows his tail."

"You must."

"And I got your bed made down too."

He grumbled and clapped her on the back as he left the stall. "Damn smarty."

"I'm the only woman you need."

"Got that right."

"And hearts are breaking all over Arizona tonight."

He threw back his head and laughed. "I'm sure they are. I'm sure they are."

CHAPTER THREE

Jake, come on," Grace half sighed and half pleaded. She was standing in his doorway staring into an abyss of clothes, books, and video game cases.

"What?" He was sprawled out on his stomach on the bed, his hands feuding over a video game controller as he shouted into a headset. His sock-covered feet kicked in the air, showing the thick black monitoring bracelet he had to wear. "We gotta blow that fucker up. No. Him. Over there, asswipe!"

"Jake!"

He turned.

"It's eleven o'clock. You need to put that away and go to bed." She motioned for him to remove the earpiece.

"You haven't even been home," he said.

"So?" She instantly felt the guilt of having gone into work and leaving him. She was pretty sure he knew it too and was playing it up.

"I'm sorry, I'm in the middle of this big new case and—"

"Seems like you just finished a big case."

"I—well, I did a couple of weeks ago and it was very important and—"

"So is this one?" He pressed pause and looked at her. His blond hair was mussed and his lips were stained red, no doubt from the bucket of Red Vines he was devouring.

"Yes."

He scowled and returned to his game. "I'll go to bed when I'm done."

"Jake—"

"Chill, Aunt Grace. Don't you have work to do or something?"

She rested her elbow on the door frame and sighed again as she rubbed her forehead.

"And will you stop sighing all the time," Jake said. "If I'm that much of a damn problem, I'll leave."

"What? No. Jesus, Jake, come on." She decided to change the subject. "Did you eat dinner?"

He held up the plastic bucket of Red Vines. There were about ten left. "Want some?"

"No. I left you a note on the fridge about the leftover spaghetti."

"Didn't want it."

"Why not?"

"Wasn't in the mood for mandolins tonight, Aunt Grace."

"So you had Red Vines?"

"Uh-huh."

"A bucket of Red Vines," she clarified.

"Not all of them. I saved you some."

"Not the point, Jake. You needed a good dinner. You're going to work hard tomorrow."

"So I'll eat a good breakfast."

"Deal. Now go to bed."

"I will soon."

"How soon?"

"Soon."

She crossed to his television and thumbed down the volume. The gunshots and explosions fell into sweet silence.

"Aunt Grace! Come on." He thumbed up the remote.

"Not too loud, I need to sleep."

"Thought you had work."

"Don't be a smart-ass."

"Better than being a dumbass."

"Jake!"

"Okay, okay." He adjusted the volume again. "How's this?"

"Good."

"Fine."

"All right. Good night."

"Night."

She closed his door and then her own as she entered her bedroom. The laptop lit up the bed, her only attentive lover as of late. She slipped out of her robe and slid beneath the covers. The soft orthopedic mattress welcomed her, as did the cool sheets and feather duvet. She wanted so badly just to lie there and allow sleep to carry her away. But the case called and she had more research to do. If she could pull off another big win, partner would be just a mere step away. She couldn't give in to fatigue now. She had to put in at least two more hours.

"I can do two hours. Hell, I've worked all night before." But it was different now with Jake. Ignoring herself and her own needs had been rather easy, but having someone else to look after was not. "I can do it, though. Sixty-hour weeks and Jake both. I'm a machine." It was what Rogers called her. A machine. He and the other partners at the firm loved her. She was their up-and-coming, their go-to girl. And she wasn't about to let that change.

Propping herself up, she reached for her laptop and notes and started in. An hour and a half later, she was fast asleep.

❖

"Jake." Grace shook him but he wouldn't budge. "Jake, for God's sake." She'd overslept by twenty minutes and Jake was passed out on the bed, his arms hanging over the side. Drool glistened on his cheek as his head rose. "Jake, get up. We're late."

"Fuck it," he said, unable to open his eyes.

"No, get up. You have to go."

"The judge can kiss it."

"They won't let you sleep in at juvie either, Jake. Now get up."

He remained still for another moment and she shook him again.

"Okay, okay."

"No okays, just get up!" She stumbled over clothes to get to his stereo. She powered it up, found heavy metal on his iPod, and slid it onto the system. Hard, heavy drums ripped through the room along with raucous guitar riffs. She turned it up louder as he covered his head with his pillow. Tearing through his dresser, she tossed a pair of jeans and a T-shirt onto the bed along with a pair of boxers and socks.

"Don't forget to brush your teeth and put on deodorant," she yelled. When she turned she was relieved to find him sitting up. She threw the stick of deodorant to him, watched him fumble for it, and hurried from the room. Thankfully, she'd taken her own shower the night before, but she still had to hurry to dress. She inhaled the scent of her lotions and perfumes as she entered her warm walk-in closet to find an outfit. They were meeting with the client today and she needed to look attractive, classic, and confident. On days like these she always went for the skirts, knowing her legs could do the job. After choosing a sleeveless white silk blouse, just-above-the-knee gray skirt, and matching short gray blazer, she took the clothes, dropped her robe, and glanced in the mirror.

"Oh," she said as she realized she had lost a little weight and a little sun from her skin. Her abdomen had the side etchings she got when she was thinner and her skin was as pale as milk. Work had kept her indoors, and coming home to Jake had kept her from her long evening walks in the setting sun. Her blond hair hung to her shoulders and her eyes looked darker than usual and fatigued. She'd have to do a great makeup job in the car this morning.

After combing her hair into a tight bun, she dressed quickly, skipping the pantyhose and opting for a short slip alone. She zipped up her skirt and buttoned her blouse, then slid into her favorite black stiletto heels to finish off her outfit. She slung her blazer over her shoulder and went to check on Jake. He was lying on his back on the bed, dressed, with his feet barely touching the floor. The music had been turned off.

"Jake," she called.

He sat up quickly and rubbed his eyes.

"Let's go."

He followed her to the kitchen.

"Did you make yourself some water like I told you to yesterday?"

"No."

She shook her head and retrieved a large personal cooler and thrust it at him to fill. "You have to do these things, Jake."

"Yeah, yeah."

She glanced at his sneakers. They were pristine white high tops.

"I told you we needed to shop and buy the right clothes and shoes; those are going to get filthy."

"The hell they will," he said. "These will be fine. Besides, I'm not some stupid cowboy. I'm not going to wear boots."

"Fine." She'd tried to get him to go shopping with her, but he had refused. She could've gone without him, but he would never wear what he didn't pick out. She'd already learned that lesson the hard way.

She headed for the car with her large shoulder bag, purse, and briefcase in hand. Breakfast was becoming a distant memory, almost as if it didn't exist anymore. The sun was just awakening, the sky still gray-blue. The neighborhood was quiet, the birds singing softly and sporadically as if they too weren't quite yet awake. Her home looked quiet with its beige stuccoed walls and dark brown tiled roof. Flagstone ran up the front column and around the two front windows. The yard was perfectly and tastefully manicured, like those of all the homes in the upscale neighborhood. She liked it but it had felt empty somehow, like the neighborhood and the house were just bones. Just material things with no meat on them and no heart within in which to beat. She tried to explain that to someone one time and got a look as if she were crazy. *Bones? Meat? What are you saying?* She'd quickly given up. But now Jake was here and things felt different. Crazy but different.

She backed out of the garage and Jake came ambling out in

baggy-waist jeans with tight fitting legs. A red ball cap sat backward on his head and he wore a different T-shirt than she'd picked out. The water cooler thumped the floor as he deposited it and climbed inside. He smelled like strong cologne.

They rode in silence for a long while and Grace found herself thinking of Ally Murphy and her offer. They'd kissed, even made out on their dates, and the physicality had been good. But Ally felt like everything else. Just bones. Just there. Still, she recalled her own pale and thinner body in the mirror and imagined Ally's long agile fingers touching her, running down her stomach to her—

Jake began to snore next to her and his music screeched from his iPod earbuds.

"What am I doing thinking about this?" She laughed a little. But, God yes, it would feel good to be touched. It had been so long. And that kiss hadn't been bad. It had been really damn nice actually. Or was it just a warm kiss from a warm, available woman?

"Does it matter?"

"Huh?" Jake startled.

"Nothing. Wake up, though. I need your help finding this place."

She pointed to the GPS screen and handed Jake the address to enter. He loved working it and sat up, interested. But to her dismay, the address didn't register.

"Where the hell is this place?" Jake asked.

She squeezed the steering wheel and exited off I-10. They turned off onto a farm road and she put the car in park. The GPS map showed nothing but unmarked land. She fumbled with the instructions she'd printed from the computer. They had four more roads to find. Dirt roads.

"Great." It was going to wreak havoc on the Mercedes.

"Where?" Jake said over his music.

"I don't know, Jake." She knew he couldn't really hear, so she said what she really thought. "Hell. It's in hell."

They continued on and Grace turned down the road as instructed by Google maps. She relaxed a little at least having found one correct road. But soon, as she turned on the next one, she knew it was wrong. They wound down a tight narrow road, bypassing sporadic homes with large gates that read no trespassing. The road ended up ahead.

"Shit, this is wrong." She followed the road to the end and made a wide turn to park. Around her she saw hawks glide through the morning sky and jackrabbits scurry about, oblivious to being hunted. Two coyotes crossed the road the way she'd come, staring at her as if they didn't have a care in the world.

"What's wrong now?" Jake came to life again.

"This road is wrong. It's a dead end."

He took the pages from her.

"Why do I always use those online maps?" she said. "And don't just take things from me."

"Why didn't you get directions from the place?" Jake asked, sifting through the papers as she fought to get them back.

"Because she was rude and she didn't seem to want to help."

"Nice. And you're sending me to this place?"

She got control of the papers.

"Juvie doesn't sound any better, does it?"

"It might."

"Don't just take things like that from me, Jake," she said again.

"I heard you."

"Don't do it."

"Why? You don't know what you're doing."

"Because it's disrespectful."

"Not that again."

"I mean it, Jake."

"Fine. But you really should know what you're doing."

She fought arguing with him and also fought the burning tears. She was doing her damn best. It wasn't her fault the map was wrong. And he wasn't the only one going to be late. At this rate, they'd be lucky to find their way back home, much less the stupid ranch.

He looked around at all the desert and stirring wildlife,

oblivious to her just like the rabbits were to the hawks. "We are in the middle of nowhere," he said in a lighter tone. "Maybe that's what you should've typed in on your MapQuest. Nowhere."

"Why? We would've just ended up here."

He looked at her and they both laughed, making her feel better.

"No, seriously, we have to get out of here," she said.

Jake shrugged. She put the car in drive.

"Lock your doors," she said, startled.

"Why?"

She pointed as a man carrying a shotgun came to stand just in front of the car. Grace felt her heart fall to her feet. "Here." She tossed Jake the phone. "Call May. Tell her we might not ever make it back into town."

Jake sank down into his seat and pressed buttons on the phone. Grace forced a smile and rolled down her window as the man, who was older, approached her door, gun lying alongside his leg. To her relief, he smiled in return.

"Oh, you're a woman. Okay," he said. "You lost?"

His teeth gleamed in the sun, but his Wranglers and boots were dusty and worn near clear through.

"Yes, I'm afraid so."

"I thought you might be a G-man or something. Out here snooping around in a fancy car."

"Nope, no G-man. Just trying to find a ranch." She laughed a little nervously.

She handed him the papers and he slid his gun beneath his arm to look.

"Aww, Healing Soul. I've heard of that place. It's nearby, but it's nowhere close."

"Sorry?"

Jake started talking to May on the phone. "May, it's Jake. We're gonna die." Grace grabbed the phone from him and threw it in the backseat.

"Can you tell us how to get there?"

He rubbed his stubbled jaw and looked to the west. "Well, like I said, it's nearby but nowhere close."

Grace cringed. *It's nearby but nowhere close. Can this morning get any worse?*

CHAPTER FOUR

There was something about April in Arizona that both awakened and soothed Madison's senses. The clusters of wildflowers bursting with rich colors saturated and stirred her vision and sense of smell, while the cool breeze easing through the trees swept through her soul like the beautiful caress of an ever-attentive lover. She loved mornings like this and often slid out of bed well before dawn just so she could sink lazily into an Adirondack chair, sip her coffee, and watch the sun rise.

All around her the desert would stretch and yawn, reaching out for mother sun. Butterflies and bees would flit and hover, the grass under her bare feet would deepen with green. The flowers would warm and send out a sharp, fresh scent. And somewhere nearby, a vocal owl would quiet and batten down for the day to sleep. The desert was magical, and each morning she was reminded why she'd chosen to open her ranch and work right here at home.

"Another day, girls, another day." Her dogs lifted their chins from the grass.

Madison scratched Beamer's head while Flaca rose and trotted to the end of the large lawn where, with nose to the ground, she began her daily search for lizards. She often found two or three and chased them intensely into the brush where she would sit and wait, head cocked, anxiously waiting for one to emerge. If Madison didn't call her away she would sit there for hours, every once in a while pawing at the edge of the brush, hoping to stir one loose. Life at the Healing Soul ranch would go on around her, horses led around the property, kids laughing, ranch hands whistling. And there would sit Flaca, oblivious to it all.

"Not today, girl," Madison said, rising from the chair. "I need all three of you today." She gave a firm whistle and they rushed onto the back patio to follow her into the house. Claws clicked on the pine floors as they hurried for the master bedroom. They were curled up on their pillow beds when she entered, one after the other, lined up near the foot of her bed, just off the large patterned rug. From there they would watch and wait as she showered and dressed. She supposed she'd be rather lonely without them, but she tried not to think of such things often.

As she emerged from the shower and dried herself, she stepped into a pair of worn but hardy jeans knowing she looked the assumed part of plain old cowgirl. With her strong build, faded T-shirts, and hiking boots, she looked to be the hard-driving blue-collar girl most people ventured she was. The blue bandana she slipped onto her head didn't help discourage that image either. But she had to be practical, and dressing comfortably and effectively like this was as much a part of her as her wine and other more expensive tastes. She enjoyed the ever-soft feel of her T-shirts and the easy pockets of her jeans, grooved and conditioned to harbor her hands and leather gloves. Her life felt the same way, grooved and conditioned, an easy fit to her habits and likes.

The dogs scrambled to their feet when she emerged from the bathroom, ready to go. The sun was angling in through the wooden blinds and haloing softly on her big bed. The covers were in a long heap in the center where she'd curled the night before, arm and leg slung like she was hugging another. It was the only way she slept comfortably, but she refused to give in and buy a body-sized pillow. Doing so, she knew, would be to admit she needed something more, and that was something a part of her wouldn't allow. She didn't need anything more. Did she?

Pushing that from her mind, she followed the dogs down the hallway to the large open kitchen where Marv was helping himself to the coffee. "You're late," he grumbled. His voice reminded her of his stubble. Ever present, somewhat whispery, and just a hint of roughness to it.

"So you keep saying," she said, refilling her mug from earlier. She snuck the cream away from him and shook it. "You used all the creamer."

He didn't blink as he took a long, loud sip from his own mug. "So you keep saying."

She smiled covertly. "Kids here yet?" Like in the bedroom, the sun was shining through the wooden blinds, encircling the nearby sunken sitting room with low-angling white light. It spread across the sofas, climbed her giant stone fireplace, and lit up the photos on her large mantel. She loved the morning light at this time of day, seemingly in sync with her routine.

Marv grumbled some more and finally answered her. "Nah."

"Then I'm not late." She squeezed his shoulder, causing him to smile. He decided to playfully attack back.

"When are you gonna fill up this fancy house with kids?"

"It's not fancy, and never."

"It is fancy, and why never?"

"It's too early for this shit, Marv."

"I know, so quit bullshitting me and tell me."

"I'll raise a family when you do."

"I got all the family I need, darlin'."

"So do I."

"Bullshit."

"It's about that time," she said, heading for the kitchen door.

"Coward."

"Old man."

He laughed and hugged her shoulders with his strong arm.

"I feed you your favorite meal, share a hundred-dollar bottle of wine, and put you up for the night, and this is how you repay me?"

"Somebody has to give you hell, and everyone else is too afraid to."

The dogs scrambled out ahead of them and Marv called after them.

"Varmints."

They followed the flagstone path along the side lawn toward the large gravel driveway and beyond that, the stables.

"They got no manners. Just like these damn kids you help."

"Well, that's why you're here, Marv. To teach them."

"There's no teachin' those dogs."

She laughed, amused, but decided to change the subject. "How are the horses this morning? That colt okay?"

"He's alive and kicking. Got a head on him. Stubborn. Not good when he's afraid too."

"Makes you wonder, doesn't it?" she asked as she strode toward the stables.

"What's that?" He kept pace next to her.

"If the owners stayed around long enough to mistreat him?"

"Wouldn't surprise me. They were probably hoping he would die too. Less guilt if he died right away, soon after the mother."

They made their way to the first stall and looked in. The colt was lying in the corner and when he saw them, he immediately jumped up and trotted nervously back and forth, keeping his distance. The few times he made eye contact, he kicked a little.

"Did he eat this morning?" she asked, even though she knew the answer.

"Hell no."

"Don't tell me you're the one who's chicken."

He didn't respond, just simply retrieved a bottle he'd obviously already filled and forced it into her hands.

"Go for it, Wonder Woman."

"No time. Kids coming." She pushed it back to him. "I just wanted a quick look-see. If anyone can do it though, you can." She grinned, knowing she was right. "It's either him or the crew. And we got a new boy coming today. Your choice." It was all bullshit. Just her giving him a hard time and vice versa first thing in the morning. In fact, if they didn't give each other a hard time, she'd wonder if he was okay.

He shook his head.

"That's what I thought." She patted his shoulder. "Good luck."

He called after her as she quickly looked in on the other horses and made her way back out of the stables. "You're gonna need help with those boys. You know it and I know it."

"So come help me." He would. He always did.

She heard him curse. "You don't pay me enough to do both."

"Then don't do both. Just worry about the colt." He'd probably been working with him for the past hour.

She heard him say something about being too old for this shit and she laughed as she crossed to the driveway. Tough as he was, there was something about the youth and innocence of wild foals that got to Marv. She knew it was similar with the boys. Only the foals seemed more helpless and they got to Marv when the kids couldn't.

Dust was kicking up in the distance as she emerged from the stables. The boys usually arrived by six forty-five per her request. She liked to clock them in at seven sharp, and sure enough, a passenger van and two SUVs trained along after one another. They always came in twos or threes because her property was so far from town, people actually felt unsure about turning in alone even with the ranch sign hanging in their face. It amused her.

She palmed the straw cowboy hat that she'd pulled off the stable nail and placed it on her head. Next came her shades, which shielded her eyes from the harsh UV rays and the dominance-seeking eyes of the troubled juveniles. Those gazes were oftentimes hotter and heavier than any penetrating Arizona sun she'd ever been under. But she held her ground well, and the less they could see of her, the less they could figure out.

She sank her hands into her pockets as the van and SUVs arrived. Dust still hung in the air behind them, almost as if it were too offended by the disturbance to settle. After ignoring a wave from a driver of one of the SUVs, she removed her hands from her pockets and crossed her arms over her chest. The dogs quickly settled at her feet, troops awaiting routine action. People crawled slowly from the vehicles. Four young teenaged boys. Two boys were from one of the local group homes. They'd been caught shoplifting together. The two others were there on similar offenses, including truancy and property destruction. One boy, however, was missing.

She checked her watch and started in, annoyed at the missing boy.

"Gather round, please," she said loudly and not overly friendly. The boys hurried directly to her, which was vastly different from their first day, when approaching her seemed to be unwritten law for "uncool." They'd shuffled slowly and indirectly, eyeing one another, none of them wanting to be the first to reach her. It was amazing what a week could do. She smiled as they all remembered to remove their ball caps and sunglasses.

"Can I work with that colt?"

"Me too!"

She held up a hand. "You will all get a chance to help with the colt. In the meantime, clock in, do your regular chores, and then report back to Marv."

They'd obviously been paying attention Friday afternoon when she'd mentioned to Marv about the arrival of the colt.

"Are we gonna have to rent a mom horse for it?" one of the boys asked.

"It would be considered a nurse mare, and no, I hope we won't have to."

The boy clutched his sack lunch to his chest. "Can he eat apples?"

"No, dumbass, he's a baby," the shortest boy said.

"Hey." She stared him down. "That's an extra day mucking stalls."

He smiled. "Okay. I mean, yes, ma'am."

The other boys laughed.

This often happened. The kids ended up loving the ranch and the work.

"If I call him a dumbass too, can I get extra duty on that colt?"

"No."

"Please?"

"You want to run laps?"

"No, ma'am."

"Then watch your mouth. Besides, the colt is too aggressive right now. But Marv's working with him. You'll all get a chance to work with him, I promise."

"I'm not a dumbass. I just thought he might like my apple. The others like apples. And carrots. And—"

"We know."

"Enough, boys. Let's go over today's agenda."

"It's the colt! That's the agenda."

"You, take a lap." She appreciated their enthusiasm, but they were getting too mouthy. His shoulders dropped along with his sack lunch. He took off around the ranch house and stables, his steel-toed work boots looking heavy. They all stood and watched, which were the rules. If one kid ran, the others either ran with him or they watched. Most hadn't run in days. They'd burned out after the first three times and decided to listen instead. It was an idea she'd taken and implemented from her friend Rob, and it was the theme of the ranch. Hard physical labor helped to tame a wild boy. Exhaust him physically and his mind will open up.

The boy bent and struggled for breath when he returned.

"You okay?" Madison asked, wanting to be sure.

"Yes, ma'am. Not as bad as that first two laps you had me do last week." He straightened and smiled at her.

"Glad to hear it. Are we ready for today's agenda yet?"

They gathered around her eagerly but another interruption approached from up the drive. A sedan was tearing up the dirt, headed directly for them. Madison watched, wondering who in the hell would drive so fast and reckless up that drive. The boys turned to watch with her.

"Who's that?"

"I'm guessing that's the new boy."

"You should make him run laps for driving like that."

She pulled off her sunglasses. "That better not be him driving. He's underage."

The car slid to a stop not ten feet from them.

"He's late. He should still run," another boy said.

The driver's door to the black Mercedes opened and a woman got out. Madison felt herself swallow with a shocking desire as the high heels and long legs were followed by a strikingly beautiful blond woman. Though coughing and waving her hands at the dust she'd raised, she was still one heck of a stunner in her tight gray skirt and matching short jacket. She struggled to walk on the gravel in her heels.

"Holy shit," a boy said softly, she wasn't sure which one. "That is one hot mama."

"Take a lap," Madison managed to say, eyes still peeled. The boys grumbled, knowing they'd have to watch him instead of the woman. "All of you take a lap."

"Aww, man."

"Make it two."

The grumbles fell away and the woman reached Madison. She stuck out her hand after tucking loose strands from her bun of blond hair behind her ears. She pulled off her sunglasses and Madison did the same. Light brown eyes met Madison's. Eyes that reminded her of a fawn's.

"You're Madison Clark?"

Madison felt a warm, pleasant jolt as their hands connected. The woman's hand was smaller but strong.

"Yes."

"Grace Hollings. And this is—"

She turned to the car but no one had budged. Instantly Madison recalled the phone call and her beating heart careened in a burning chest.

"You're late," Madison said.

Grace turned back to her. "Am I?"

"Yes. Don't let it happen again." She was struggling for control and she automatically went on the attack, too afraid to be friendly.

"I got lost. Can't I get a mulligan or something?" She smiled, but it was tight with noticeable aggression.

"We don't play golf around here, but you just got it."

"Okay, then." She turned back to the car and yelled. "Jake! Get out here!" The car door slowly opened and Grace turned and was speaking to her again. "You wouldn't believe the morning we've had. Damn online maps led us five miles the wrong way. We ran into a man protecting his land with a gun. This place is in the middle of nowhere. Honestly, it's a pain in the ass to get out here."

Madison wasn't sure what to say. Was this supposed to be her fault? And a man with a gun? What? She had several herself and most folks did out here, but Grace sounded like he was threatening.

She steeled her jaw. "Now you know. You can plan better next time. And maybe avoid the man with the gun?"

"Are you some kind of rude cowgirl or something?" She glared at her with those eyes like golden molasses.

Ouch. Madison clenched her jaw and considered sparring with her. Instead, she found herself blinking in disbelief. No parent had ever readily been so rude to her. Grace Hollings continued.

"Well, I'm an attorney and my nephew is court ordered to be here. Otherwise I—"

"Would have him somewhere closer to home. Got it." Madison strode quickly up to Jake, who had finally emerged from the vehicle. He stood looking at her with unaffected eyes, baggy jeans, high top sneakers, and a T-shirt. "Jake, I'm Madison Clark. Welcome to H and S. Take a lap."

"What?" He eyed the boys who were running nearby. "Why?"

"Because you're late."

"That's not my fault!"

"Doesn't matter."

"Aunt Grace!" He stormed up to her. "Tell her it's not my fault."

"It really isn't. We got lost."

"You had directions."

Grace shook her head quickly. "I had Internet directions."

"You were sent directions from me via e-mail. There is also a map on the brochure."

"Fine, whatever. It's my fault, not his."

"Doesn't matter." She walked up to them. "Before you run, take off your iPod and get rid of your phone. Neither one is allowed here. And I hope you brought pants that fit and steel-toed boots. They were on the list."

"Aunt Grace!" he said again.

Grace held out her hands for his iPod and phone and said, "I will buy you the stuff tonight. I tried to tell you yesterday, but you refused to listen."

"Because this is some bullshit!"

"That's two laps," Madison said loudly.

The other boys finished their run and came in breathing heavily. They gave Jake the once-over and slowly shook their heads. Jake stuck out his chest even though he looked as though he might break down and cry.

"Boys, go start in on your morning chores and then report to Marv."

"Yes, ma'am," they said in unison, picking up their lunches as they went.

"Listen, Ms. Clark," Grace started.

Madison stood staring at Jake, who finally took off, running at a slow pace. She watched him closely, knowing she hadn't reached him. Not by a long shot. But he didn't cry. He never wiped his face. Not once.

"I'm sorry about today. I tried to get him up on time. Tried to buy him the things you requested—"

"Then why didn't you?"

"Because—" She sighed. "Jake's difficult. It's why he's here."

"Who's the adult? You or him?"

"I am, but—"

"No buts. He either shows up on time with the proper attire or he's out."

"He's court ordered—"

"I will report it as a fail to complete the program to the judge."

"Over shoes?"

"And pants and time? Yes. I've done it before."

"I would love to see that. Especially since I know the judge."

They stared at each other and Madison was angry, not just at

Grace's attitude but because she found her physically attractive. How could she have been drawn to such a woman? And why the hell couldn't she make it stop?

"Then maybe you two can work something else out." Yes, get rid of her. Either for the day or for good. Then Madison could get a hold of herself.

Grace crossed her arms and stood like Madison. Guarded. "We may have to."

They watched Jake run and walk and run and walk. When he finally finished he stumbled up to them and retched. Grace hurried to the car and retrieved a large canister of water.

"You're lucky I at least insisted on this," she said, handing it over.

He took a swig and fingered an obvious stitch in his side. "That sucked. This place sucks."

"Would you like to do another?"

He spit. "No way. You can forget it."

"Then watch your mouth."

He glanced at Grace. "Can't we just go? Fuck this place. It smells, she's evil, and it's in the middle of the damn desert."

Grace looked away, obviously uncomfortable.

"I don't have any more time to waste," Madison said. She began to walk away.

"Wait. Ms. Clark, please. Wait."

Madison heard the heels crunch on gravel and she slowed and turned. Grace fell in one swift motion, one leg kicked up followed quickly by the other. Madison reached out and caught her arm just in time. She lifted her up easily and steadied her.

"Jesus," Grace muttered and straightened her clothing. "Ever hear of concrete?" When Madison didn't respond, she said with hesitation, "Thanks."

Madison nodded, fighting a flush. Grace was lithe and warm, and she could smell her now. Gardenia and something warmer, darker, something stroking her insides probably much like the way Grace's long, delicate fingers would feel.

"I need Jake to be here. He—I—" She sighed again. "He's been with me for six months and I can't get a handle on him. He always seems to be in trouble and he won't listen to anything I say. It's either here or juvenile detention, and I don't want to see him end up there. He's a good kid, my flesh and blood, and I just—"

"Need help."

Her eyes shot to Madison's. "Yes."

Madison had heard this all before, but usually she could see through it for what it was. Most parents in these situations just wanted to hand off their kid, completely helpless and hopeless. And while Grace hinted at that, Madison hoped for that spark of love she heard in her voice when she referred to Jake as flesh and blood. That spark of love would be their starting point, their foundation for which everything else was built, torn down, and built again.

"Get him over here."

Jake approached them slowly, red faced, still sucking on the water.

"Yeah?"

Madison started in. "Time is of the essence around here. So arrive fifteen minutes before clock-in every morning. That means six forty-five. If you're late, you run. One lap for every minute."

"But—"

"No buts. Also, when you speak to any adult around here, you respond with ma'am or sir, and you always remove your hat and sunglasses to do so." She waited for him to get the hint. Grace had to tell him and he scoffed as he removed his hat.

"This shows respect, and you should do it for any adult. In order to get respect from me or the other staff, however, it has to be earned."

He wouldn't look at her for very long, just shifted his weight and spat.

"You can choose to obey these rules or not. If you don't obey the rules, you run."

"What if I refuse to run?"

"Then you're out. Might as well leave now."

"Okay, then."

"Jake—wait. Jake, you have to stay. It's either this or juvie."

"I don't care." But Madison could see that the thought troubled him a little.

"If you don't want to run my program, then you can leave. Either with her, or if she refuses to allow you to leave, you can walk. But it's miles and miles to town. And it's hot today. And I promise you that if you go on your own, the sheriff will be notified and you will be considered AWOL and you will be arrested."

Grace gasped and fingered her delicate-looking throat. "Jake, you need to stay."

"Fine. Jesus Christ."

"Take a lap."

"What? Hey, fuck you."

"That's another."

"I can't run that long!"

"I'm not quite finished." She eyed the stables where the other boys milled about doing their chores. Marv was showing one boy how to properly bathe a small pony.

"See that man? That's Marv. After you go over the agenda with me every morning, you will clock in with Marv in the stables and clock out there every evening. Now, Marv's as mean and as tough as he looks, just as I am. So we are not to be disobeyed under any circumstances. These horses you will be working with are special. They've been hurt, abused, abandoned, and neglected. Some are sick. Some are weak. All need to be treated with respect and dignity. They need your kindness and empathy just as much as they need your constant attention."

He grimaced but then softened ever so slightly. "Really? They've been hurt?"

It was what she loved to see. The boy had hope, and it had just showed itself.

"Some of them, yes. So I'm very protective of them and I need you to be too."

He pressed his lips together but didn't respond. Finally, he nodded.

"Welcome to Healing Soul. Get started on those laps."

"Excuse me?" Grace asked as Jake took off in a slow trot. "What exactly will he be doing?"

"You didn't read the brochure or the e-mails?" Grace was seriously wasting her time and seriously stirring her in ways she found unsettling and concerning.

"I did, but could you go over it? Will he—get hurt?"

"Not if he follows the rules. And you signed the injury waiver."

"And what are the rules? Exactly?"

"Jake will learn them today."

Grace gave a pleasant but obviously frustrated laugh. "Can't I know them?"

"You sure can. Jake should be able to recite them when you pick him up at four. Now, if you'll excuse me, I have a ranch to run."

"What about lunch?" Grace asked. "I have it in the car. Will he get a chance to eat it?"

"Lunch is at eleven sharp. As written in the brochure and e-mails you should've received, if your child brought lunch it will be stored in a cooler for him until time to eat. If he didn't, then he can eat our lunch for three dollars and fifty cents. Water is the only drink allowed and they are permitted to drink that throughout the day. They have the option of iced tea at lunch."

"No Monster? Or Rockstar?" She laughed but stopped when Madison didn't. "Right. Okay."

Madison turned, having had enough. "See you at four sharp."

"About that. I have to work late some days and can't—"

"Four sharp."

Grace growled, "Yes, ma'am," and stormed off to the car. She retrieved a sack lunch and left it next to Jake's water. Then, "What if Jake gets hurt?"

"I have your number on file. We will call you."

Madison often wondered where these concerned parents were when their kids were breaking and entering or stealing cars or skipping school. Where was Grace? In court? With clients? At happy hour? She made a mental note to go over Jake's file again. She wanted and needed to know more.

"Have a nice day." Madison tilted her hat at Grace and headed off toward the stables. Jake followed, having finished his laps. Lila greeted him and then ran to Grace, who was walking stiffly to her car. The dog sat and watched as she sped away, and Madison wondered if there was any herding possible when it came to Jake and Grace Hollings.

CHAPTER FIVE

I just met the devil," Grace said as she finally pulled onto the highway to speed away from the ranch. "And ugh, she lives in hell!" She eased down her window, feeling like she needed to be windblown free of dust.

"Calm down, now what? You met the devil?" It was May, Grace's good friend and longtime colleague. Her voice was loud and clear throughout the car, coming through the speakers. Grace had called her to tell her she was running late.

"That ranch I had to take Jake to? She runs it, and she's a nightmare."

"She? Is she cute?"

"Stop it."

"She's got you all worked up. She must be."

"She's rude."

"And you're not? Please, Grace Marie. You make stone-cold judges pee their gowns."

"That isn't hard to do."

"Ha. Anyway, when will you be here? We need to get ready for that client meeting."

"Give me forty-five minutes. I'm out near freakin' Tonopah."

"You got it. Is she dark? The devil woman? I know you love those brunettes. And if she's tall I don't care if she is Satan, even you wouldn't be able to resist."

"Good-bye, May." She ended the call and rolled up her windows.

As she finger-styled the loose strands of her hair she began to talk to herself, just as she often did on the way into work. Only today, her self-monologue didn't have anything to do with work or with Jake.

"So she's attractive. So are wild animals. Doesn't mean anything. So she has incredible arms and legs and eyes..." She shook her head. "Her mouth is awful. So rude. And those clothes? Good grief, has she been dragged behind her horses? Still, they fit her nicely and the work must be dirty. Ugh, she probably eats with her bare hands, picks her teeth with a knife, and scratches herself at least three times a day in front of others. Hmm...I'd like to see that. She does have a nice tush." She glanced at herself in the rearview mirror. "Did I just say *tush*? God, I'm losing it. Get a grip, Grace." She laughed softly.

Get a grip, Grace. That was Gabby's favorite saying.

Grace felt her mood change as if clouds had rolled in over the Mercedes. She felt gray, more so than usual. Gabrielle was in rehab for the third time. Grace hoped it was her final time. She and Jake couldn't take much more. Heroin was a monster and it had stolen Gabby years ago. And honestly, Grace didn't know how Jake had survived it all as well as he had. She should've visited more, insisted that Gabby and Jake come stay with her. She would've at least been able to keep a better eye on both of them. But Gabby had been stubborn, staying in Ohio up until six months ago when child protective services called Grace to inform her that Jake was under their care and that Gabby was missing.

"I don't know how he made it," she said softly. "Poor Jake. She just took off. I mean, she just up and took off. Or maybe she just didn't come home. I don't know. I'll probably never know. It's possible Gabby doesn't even know. It doesn't matter now anyway. I went and got Jake. The P.I. found Gabby. She's in rehab. Mom is in denial as usual. I'm taking care of things. Should've done a better job, but what else is new? Gabby cleans up her mess when I visit and then makes a new one as soon as I'm gone. Been that way for years. I should've just taken Jake. Despite his refusal to come with me. I should've just taken him and sued for custody. Mom wasn't going to do anything and Gabby wouldn't have stopped me." She grew quiet for a moment. "He would've run away. That's exactly what he would've done." A long sigh escaped her and she remained silent for the rest of her journey.

When she reached her office building, she still felt dirty, so she strolled inside the large, overly pale yellow ladies' room and groaned at her reflection.

"No wonder the cowgirl was so rude. I look like a dolled-up troll." With a quick jerk of her fingers, she released her blond mane and brushed it, then tied it in a tight bun. She rinsed her face and redid her makeup. Then she brushed off her clothes and sprayed on some perfume. Feeling only half-troll, she finally left the restroom and headed for her office. Staff greeted her, as did a few of the partners. The day appeared to already be in full swing and she felt a little sheepish walking in after eight.

"Tardy points," May said, swiveling around in Grace's desk chair.

"I know, I know." Grace closed her door and inhaled the warm vanilla scent of her office. "I avoided eye contact out there like I'd shot my couch or something this morning."

"Your couch?"

"Yeah, you know. Shot something and felt guilty over it?"

"Never heard that one."

"Well, I wasn't about to say dog, now was I?"

"Ugh, you just did." May slid binders around and thumped a pencil on a yellow legal pad. "You look dashing as always. Definitely ranch attire."

"Shut up. I actually liked this outfit before today." She slid off her jacket and rubbed her bare arms. Her cardigan felt inviting and safe as she slipped it over her shoulders. "Oh God, my shoes." She took them off and retrieved a cloth from her desk drawer. She polished them quickly and then glided them back onto her feet. "Nearly ruined them. She's got the whole drive in gravel. Gravel! Of all things. And all the damn roads are dirt."

"It's a ranch, Grace, not a country club."

"Coffee?" Janine, Grace's secretary, cracked the door to ask.

"Yes, please."

"Not for me, thanks!" May called out, knowing damn well that Janine wasn't offering. "So the ranch was nice?"

"Not now, May. God, I don't want to think about it."

"But you felt okay leaving Jake there?"

Grace shooed her from her chair and May dragged over a client chair to sit across from her.

"I guess. I mean, it wasn't bad. It was a ranch. Sort of beautiful in a working kind of way. It was just the owner. Ms. Clark."

"Ms. Clark? Sounds so formal."

"She is, kind of. I don't know. I have other things to think about right now, okay? Jake has to be there. There's not really anything I can do about it. Ms. Clark seemed very organized and capable. And according to Judge Newsom, she knows her stuff and her program is highly effective."

"Okay, we'll drop it. It's just that crazy voicemail Jake left." She laughed. "I think I'll be laughing at that for the rest of the week." When Grace didn't respond she added, "And you sounded so worked up over the phone. I really thought someone finally got your goat."

Had she? Grace hesitated in responding. If so, why? Because Madison was so assertive and didn't seem the least bit unsure or friendly? She'd dealt with people like that before. Every day, in fact. So what was the deal? It was because she wasn't friendly. That was it. She didn't even try to be polite to Grace. Most people in that situation would've. Wouldn't they? Most people were nice to her and even a little impressed by her. But Madison Clark couldn't have cared less, and *that* was what was bothering her. Her blatant disregard.

"Coffee, coffee, coffee," Janine said as she entered.

"Oh, thank God." She needed the lift and the interruption.

"Say, Janine," May started. "Can I get a Diet Pepsi?"

Janine huffed and eyed Grace. "Please?" Grace asked.

Another huff and Janine exited.

"You have your own secretary, you know," Grace said, sipping her coffee with just the perfect amount of cream.

"I know. But I like Janine because she likes me so much."

"You're harassing her and you love it. Weren't you shown empathy as a child, May?"

"Apparently not. And Joe's boring with a capital *B*. No reaction at all from that slug on a rug. He just hums into his head set and files his nails. I wish we could trade. Janine's feisty."

"Janine's an angel, and you keep your claws off her."

"Bor-ing." She made a *b* with her hands. "So anyway, let's talk shop."

"Let's."

"We need to start with our points."

"Shoot." But Grace spaced out as May started in. Her vision went to the photo on her bookshelf of Gabby and Jake. She hoped Jake was faring well, and she hoped for his sake that Madison Clark's rehabilitating horse ranch was all it was hyped up to be, because she was losing him. He was slipping away just like Gabby. Gabby was about thirteen when she first started down that dangerous road. It had started with skipping school, then cigarettes, then pot. Soon it was speed and then finally, heroin. Grace refused to stand by and watch Jake go down the same path. Just because their mother didn't do anything but drown herself in her sorrows and denial with vodka, it didn't mean she was going to mentally check out. No, sir. Jake was her nephew and he deserved better. Gabby did too. She just couldn't see it yet.

"You want to write this down?"

"Huh?" She snapped back in. "I thought you were."

"Wait, I've got some notes on my laptop. Be right back."

May vanished out the door and Grace opened her desk drawer and fished out two aspirin to chew. Then she rose and touched the picture of Gabby and Jake. "Come back to us, Gabby, I can't do this alone."

❖

Later that afternoon, Grace was weaving through traffic on I-10, heading west out toward Tonopah to pick up Jake. She was pushing in on four o'clock and she wasn't sure how in the world she was going to do this every day. She and May had really been on a roll with research when she'd glanced at the clock and found it was already after three. May had not been happy and neither had she, but what was she supposed to do? Up until Jake's arrival, her career had been everything. Ten years of that had helped her to become quite the young attorney, and making partner was definitely in her near future. If she could just hang on and get Jake on track.

"Who am I kidding? I'll never be able to work like that with Jake at home. How would that be fair to him? I might as well be strung out on heroin for all he knows. What's the difference? An absent parent is an absent parent."

How many times a day did she pray to Gabby? Nine? Ten? She just needed her to kick in so badly. Jake was suffering and he was out of control. Skipping school, fighting, refusing to listen. And walking out of restaurants without paying? What the hell? Where did he learn such behavior? Even at thirteen, Gabby never stole. At least not to her knowledge.

"He won't listen." She'd tried having normal face-to-face conversations. She'd tried lecturing. She'd tried yelling. Nothing worked. And grounding him only pissed him off to the point of just walking out and not returning until the following day, leaving her a nervous wreck all night long.

"If this doesn't work, I don't know what I'll do." She wrung her hands on her steering wheel and pulled off the interstate. She sped until she came upon the road to the ranch. Tires kicking up dirt, she continued to speed until she reached the entrance. White fences lined the property, and a beautiful hanging cast iron sign said *Healing Soul Ranch.*

It blew slightly in the wind as she drove past. "Phew. Made it." She laughed at how ridiculously worried she was over it. But then she remembered Jake having to run and she wondered if the same thing applied when the day ended. She sped up just in case and was suddenly very worried at what she'd find. Would Jake be near death? Covered in dirt and sweat, having run miles and miles for disobedience? Would his clothes be torn? Would he be dehydrated?

Would he refuse to come back? She exhaled long and slow and tried to calm her nerves. Instead, she focused on the beauty of the ranch.

Despite the dirt and first hurried appearances, it was quite beautiful. Many different trees lined the drive, along with groups of lush-looking wildflowers. Huge oaks shaded the large house as she neared the driveway. The house looked like a ranch home and appeared to be made of wood. But its huge picture windows and glossy finish spoke of more expensive tastes, as did the large deck leading out from the side door. It held a weighty-looking chiminea, cast iron furniture with modern cushions and designs. Numerous healthy green plants were growing in large ceramic pots, and she had the urge to curl there on that deck in her bare feet and watch the sunset with a bottle of wine.

The thought drifted away, though, as she turned off the engine and climbed from the car. Vibrant grass edged the driveway and led to the stables, which were designed to match the house and were nearly as big. Flagstone paths wound here and there throughout the property and led to the holding pens behind the house and stables. There she saw boys huddled around something and she quickly slipped off her shoes and followed the path up to the rails. The same white dog she'd seen that morning trotted up to her and smelled her legs. Grace gave her a quick pat and saw two other dogs with similar builds lying near the boys at the pen. No one looked at her when she approached. Not even Jake, though she could tell her presence was sensed. The boys remained fixated, most of them dirty and sweaty, arms and legs hanging off the bars of the pen. They looked worn out but serious.

"Now, since he won't eat, we gotta try it this way."

A gruff but nice-looking cowboy was huddled over a baby horse. He held the horse's head between his legs and dipped his fingers in milk. Then he forced them in the baby's mouth. The horse tried to fight it at first, but then, after two more tries with fresh dips, he began to suckle.

"What we did was we kept the milk from him for a few hours so he was good and hungry. Then we introduced the milk with fingers. Fingers are warm and natural feeling. Once he gets used to the fingers, then we reintroduce the bottle. Let's hope it works. Jake? You wanna unscrew that bottle and dip the nipple in the milk?"

"Aww, man. He gets to do it?" a boy said.

"Dang, man."

"He's new. This is his trial by fire," the cowboy said. "If the horse doesn't take the nipple, then Jake has to run."

Jake frowned. "Seriously?"

"Nah, I'm kiddin', kid."

To her amazement, Jake then eagerly climbed through the bars and did as instructed. Sweat tracked through the dirt on his skin from his temples, leading down to his jawline. His neck was red, along with his ears. His clothes were filthy and his once-pristine white shoes were long ago beaten by dirt. But he looked healthy, vibrant, alive. She smiled.

"Good, now hand me that bottle."

The cowboy placed the nipple in the horse's mouth along with his fingers, which the baby continued to suck on. He let him do this a few more times, dipping it along with his fingers. The horse continued suckling and the cowboy quickly screwed on the bottle and returned the nipple to the horse's mouth. The baby hesitated ever so slightly, but with the help of the cowboy's finger once again, the horse began to guzzle the bottle.

Grace was so thrilled to see it happen she clapped.

The boys all turned to look at her and the cowboy grimaced.

"Keep quiet. Don't wanna spook him."

"Sorry," she said and nearly felt herself blush.

"What are you doing here?" Jake asked, coming to stand at the barred fence. He didn't look happy to see her.

"It's almost four."

His brown eyes fell. "Oh."

Suddenly a cowbell rang behind them. The boys unwrapped themselves from the fence and trotted over to the stables. Madison Clark stood there with a clipboard. Grace approached slowly, curious. She saw a large whiteboard hanging on the stable wall. It reminded the boys of clock-in time and to be sure and check with

Marv before starting chores. Beneath that it said every boy must have permission before moving a horse from one place to another.

She listened as Madison called out names to give the go-ahead to clock out. The boys clapped softly as each name was called. A few of the vehicles Grace had seen that morning had arrived. After the boys clocked out, they said their good-byes and walked slowly to their vehicles, crawled inside like they were tired, and drove away. Jake was the only boy left standing.

"Great," she said as she walked over. The flagstone path felt warm on her feet to the point where she almost relaxed. But then Madison looked up and her face showed surprise and then… nothing.

"Ms. Hollings."

"I'm on time," she said cheerfully and then felt like a fool.

"Yes, you are." She lowered the clipboard and Grace noticed the sweat lining the blue bandana around her head. Grace wondered what color her hair was. It was difficult to tell from under the cover of her hat and bandana. But what she could see looked to be a light brown. It curled up a bit on her neck so she knew it was cut short. The thought quickened her heart rate as the very real possibility that Madison Clark could be gay made itself known.

She continued to take her in carefully, acting as if she were casually glancing around. The sun had baked Madison's neck to a dark golden brown, and her arms looked somehow stronger than before and her legs thicker with muscle. Maybe it was because the jeans looked slightly damp, as if she'd recently run through a mist. Maybe she had been bathing horses. The thought of Madison all wet and glistening in the sunlight caused Grace to quiver with sudden desire.

"How did he do?" Grace asked hesitantly, fearing the answer but needing to focus on something else, and quickly. She squeezed Jake's arm but he pulled away and spat, then covered it with dirt with his shoe.

"I'm afraid I can't give Jake credit for today," Madison said, but she didn't sound sad or disappointed. Just very matter-of-fact, like she had been that morning.

"What does that mean?" Grace wondered how she did it. All these kids, their behavior and emotions. How did she stay so professional and detached? Even Grace lost herself to passion when trying some cases. Of course she always played it to her advantage, but still. She had sleepless nights; she had splinters of things she'd witnessed fester under her skin. Did Madison?

Jake too seemed unaffected. He kicked the ground. Was Grace the only one on earth who gave a damn?

Grace rubbed her temples in frustration. "Tell me what that means, please." She sounded weak, wounded, and she didn't like exposing that to Madison Clark.

"He didn't complete his chores."

"Maybe he didn't know how."

"He was shown how."

"Oh." Grace looked at him. "Jake?"

"I just didn't feel like doing it."

"But what about that baby horse? I saw you help feed it. That was awesome."

"He fed the colt?" Madison asked.

"He helped the cowboy."

"The colt ate?" Madison asked Jake.

He nodded. "Yes, ma'am. He ate from the bottle. He's eating now."

Madison sighed with obvious relief. "Well, then. That's good news. Did you like working him? That colt?"

Again, Jake nodded.

Madison scribbled on her clipboard, then flapped it against her thigh. "You get some credit for today for helping with the colt. But tomorrow you need to do better. If you do, you get to help some more with that foal. Sound good?"

He nodded.

"Excuse me?"

"Yes, ma'am."

"Very good. Go home, eat well, and get some rest. And tomorrow I expect you to be prepared with the proper attire and attitude."

"Yes, ma'am."

"Have a good night, then." She smiled very briefly and Grace felt her breath catch. *Oh my. She's really gorgeous when she smiles.*

Grace forced herself to look away. "Good night." Did Madison Clark have manners after all? Or worse, had she had them all along but didn't feel that Grace was worthy of them?

Who cares? "God, why do I give a damn?"

"Huh?"

"Nothing. Get in the car."

"You're wondering why you give a damn about me, aren't you?" Jake asked, anger crowning his brow.

"What? No. Jake, no, of course not."

He climbed from the car and began to walk quickly down the dirt drive. Grace hurriedly reversed, turned, and drove alongside him. She powered the window down.

"Jake, please."

"Shut up. Just shut up."

"Jake, I wasn't talking about you. I swear."

"Then who were you talking about?"

He wiped tears with the back of his wrist. Grace slammed on her brakes and jumped from the car. She hurried around the front and embraced him hard. He tried to pull away, but she held on tightly and whispered in his ear.

"I would never, ever say or even think that about you. Do you understand? I was talking about the cowgirl. Ms. Clark."

He pulled away and sniffled. But then spat and shuffled his feet to look tough. "What about her?"

Grace glanced back at the ranch and saw Madison and the cowboy watching. They were out of earshot but looked very concerned.

"She's been kind of rude to me today and I asked myself why I gave a damn. Who cares if she's rude to me? She's just a woman."

Jake stared at her. "Really?"

"Yes, Jake. It had nothing to do with you."

"Even though I fucked up today?"

"Yes. And watch your mouth or I'll make you run laps."

He laughed.

"Now can we go home before she comes over here and makes us both run?"

"Yeah." He returned to the car and they both eased inside. "I've had enough running today."

"I bet."

"I can't wait to get home and play video games. I'm going to play *Call of Duty* all night long."

"You have to get up early again."

"So?"

"And we have shopping to do."

"Aw, come on. Take me home and you can shop."

"Oh, no. You're coming with. If I have to suffer through shopping for pants that fit you, you darn well are going to suffer with me." She reached over and squeezed his hand. He quickly moved it to his lap and powered his seat back.

"Whatever. I'm still playing *Black Ops* when we get home."

"So did you like the place?"

"No."

"Not at all?"

"Well, the horses were cool." He perked up a little. "They have a donkey. A little horse, you know? His name is Speedy and he only has one eye."

"Poor thing."

"No, it's cool because he doesn't seem to notice. He does everything fine. At least now he does. I guess at first he was injured and starved and stuff. But he's okay now. He loves apples. I thought he was going to eat my hand."

"Sounds like fun. I would love to feed him."

"He's a total pig. He follows you around and around and nudges you until you feed him. So we have to make him walk a lot until we give in. Plus it's like physical therapy for him too. He goes in a pool-like thing every other day for his hips, to exercise."

"Wow, sounds like they know what they're doing."

"Yeah, I guess."

"So what are the rules?"

He was busy biting a cuticle but his body went slack and thumped against the chair as if she'd just sucked the life from him. "Really?"

"Really. I want to know."

He sighed and began counting them off. "No lying, no stealing, no running off, no disobeying, no arguing, no fighting, no hurting or neglecting the animals, no cell phone or any electronic equipment, no cussing, no bullying."

"That all?"

"No caffeine or sugary drinks. Only on special occasions."

"What about the iced tea?"

"She said tea doesn't have enough caffeine to hurt us. And we're only allowed tea at lunch. It's water the rest of the time. Oh, and tomorrow I want to buy lunch. Marv and Bobby cook out on the grill and make hamburgers and chicken and stuff. Smelled so good."

"Made my peanut butter and jelly taste pretty lame, huh?"

He nodded. "Can I have McDonald's for dinner? I'm starved."

"Sure. But after we shop." She had a feeling he'd pass out as soon as he ate, despite his desire for video games.

After what seemed like a very long drive back toward home, she pulled into a shopping plaza and entered a store to find him jeans. He whined and complained when he tried them on. They didn't hang low enough in the crotch and they weren't tight enough at the ankles. He'd look like a newb. Whatever a newb was. But she reminded him of the running and he finally slumped his shoulders and agreed. She bought him five pair and a pair of steel-toed work boots from the shoe store next door. He also picked out a few new ball caps and some white T-shirts. By the time they finished it was after six and he ate his Big Mac and fries on the way home and fell asleep as they pulled into the drive. Grace helped him inside, led him to his bed, and watched as he collapsed onto the rumpled bedspread. Carefully, she removed his shoes and dirty socks, baggy pants and shirt. He was filthy but she didn't have the heart to wake him. So she left him sleeping, set his alarm, and went to wash his new clothes.

Morning would come soon enough, and somehow, washing his clothes and tidying up after him around the house soothed her enough to make her want to fall asleep as well. But she had more research and fine points to go over for that case. Her night, unfortunately, was just beginning. And she wondered, not for the first time, how many other parental guardians' nights were just beginning too.

CHAPTER SIX

"So you got him to eat, huh?" Rob Sheffield asked, coming up on the pen. He rested his chin on his hands and grinned at Madison and the colt. "Handsome little guy."

"Marv did it. As always. He bitches and moans, but he loves these animals just as much as I do," Madison said.

"The boys too," he replied.

"I suppose."

"Don't even deny it. We all know you care about these boys. Probably more than their damn parents do."

"That's a sad statement."

"It's true. We all know the world would be a better place if more parents gave a damn." He pushed off from the pen and came around inside. The colt had finished eating, and he trotted away from Rob when he saw him.

"Still skittish."

"A bit."

Rob stood calmly and held out his palms from his sides. He ticked softly, and eventually the colt came up and sniffed him. When Rob tried to pet him on the flank, though, he bolted, causing Rob to laugh. Being a big guy at six foot five and 240 pounds, Rob's size was formidable and his laughter deep and resounding. The colt kicked and continued to run.

"He likes you," Madison said.

"I don't think so."

"He doesn't come up to anyone else to check them out."

"Well, you got to know what to say." He laughed as the colt came again to briefly nudge his palm. "How's he been? Any teeth grinding or salivating?"

"No."

"Rolling around or abdominal sensitivity?"

"Don't think so."

"You want to hold him while I check him out?"

Madison bent to hold him tightly. He resisted at first, but when Rob offered his palm, he quieted.

"That's a boy. So handsome. Loving that star there, boy," Rob whispered.

"He is beautiful, isn't he?"

"Sure is. That pretty brown all over. He's a looker. Especially with that white star." Rob went silent as he listened with a stethoscope. He pressed it against his chest, then his abdomen, checking both sides. He used his fingers to gently feel his midsection, then examined his teeth and feet. He also checked his ears and eyes.

"Well, he looks okay. How's his stool? Normal?"

"Yeah."

"And the rescue gave him colostrum and had him on an IV for a few days?"

"Yes."

"I'll check his immunity level, but I don't see any sign of neonatal diseases. I think he just got uncomfortable and refused to eat. You do need to keep him with that mare, though."

"He's been sleeping with her. He kept trying to feed from her for a while, but now that he's eating from the bottle he should be fine. We'll keep him with her until he needs his human time."

"I knew you knew what you were doing."

"Ha, thanks."

"He'll be okay."

"Glad to know you know what you're doing," she said with a grin.

"Madness is such a smart-ass." He brushed his hands on his

pants. She rolled her eyes at the nickname he'd given her back in college. They'd both been studying psychology and he found the pun quite funny. Now anyone who knew her well used it, much to her chagrin.

"You going to offer me some wine or what?" he asked with a sheepish grin.

Madison slipped a light noose around the colt's neck and walked with Rob to the stables. The day was settling in for the night and the breeze had grown a bit cooler. It blew through the trees with a gentle rustle and tickled the colt's ears. It was a perfect evening for sharing wine with a friend.

She entered the stall with the colt and Rob stood petting Mazey on the snout, whispering, "Hey, girl, how's that skin, huh?" He stroked her long and soft, and her back shuffled under his hands in approval.

"She's been doing okay. The boys bathe her carefully every day and apply the medication. And she gets her soaks and gets covered in the sun."

"Good, good."

Madison released the colt and watched as he trotted the length of the stall and then settled in the corner. "I was hoping he would bond with Mazey, but he seems to be quite the rebel without a cause."

"Mazey's a lover. She'll win him over." He grew serious for a moment and Madison inhaled the deep scents of the stable. The stables were quiet and still with the occasional whistle of the wind coming through a crack in the door. In the distant tall corner a large fan blew fresh air for the horses. If she had wanted she could've curled up next to the colt and fallen fast asleep, inhaling the scents and listening to the hum and whistle.

"Have the boys asked what happened to Mazey yet?"

The thought of Mazey and her trauma snapped her out of her pleasant daze.

She leaned in and kissed Mazey on the nose. "They have. But I don't answer. I think they know, though. It's pretty obvious."

She hated to think about it herself and mostly refused to anymore. Mazey was okay now, and with her daily skin care routine, she was close to thriving. That was all that mattered now.

"It's amazing how she isn't afraid anymore," Rob said softly.

"Yes, it is."

"Huh, Mazey girl? You're a good girl."

"Come on, let's get some wine before you sweet-talk that horse to death."

Rob laughed and followed her out after switching on several more fans. The days were getting warmer, and Madison made sure her horses were well ventilated while in the stables at night. If she slept comfortably, she made damn sure her horses did as well. She looked back on the stables as they reached the patio. Some called her obsessive-compulsive when it came to the horses, but she just called it being a good parent. She'd long to check on them again before bed. Question was, could she resist?

Once inside the house she and Rob removed their shoes in the mudroom. Madison removed her socks as well and slid into her favorite slippers. Rob followed her to the kitchen, watched her retrieve two heavy wineglasses, and then moved into the sunken sitting room to settle on the sofa.

"Did you eat yet?" She needed to know in order to pick the perfect wine for the moment.

"Yes." He groaned as he sank into the sofa.

"Good, do you want some dessert? I have chocolate and the perfect wine to go with it."

"Sounds good."

She opened the wine cooler and pulled out the bottle of Chateau La Mission Haut-Brion '07. It wasn't one of her older, more expensive wines, but she'd been dying to try it. He took his glass with a broad grin and a thank you.

She placed her own glass on the coffee table and slid him the box of Swiss chocolate. Usually she would shower before cuddling up in her satin robe to enjoy the wine, but her friends sometimes stopped by for some after-dinner vino and she loved the company and conversation.

"I always feel like I'm messing up your couch with all my dust," Rob said, helping himself to a small wedge of chocolate.

"Don't be ridiculous. I picked out this sofa set with my ranch hands in mind." She smiled. "Besides, it's leather. I just wipe the dust right off." She was quite dirty herself and usually was after walking through thick dirt, dust, and Bermuda hay all day. But she straightened up nightly after her shower, and if guests had come, she simply wiped down the couches.

"Still."

"Just relax." She sat back with wine and chocolate in hand, tucking her feet up under her legs. First she took a generous bite of chocolate, let it melt in her mouth, and then she stirred her wineglass, inhaled, and noticed the coffee and berry aromas. She sipped and allowed the flavors to play. They came at once as she swished a little and then swallowed. Mahogany, berry, vanilla, and yes, a bit of a chocolate aftertaste. Perfection.

"This is good stuff," he said, taking his own hearty sip. "Very nice. All that's missing is a good man."

"You have one."

"Please."

"You're saying Juan doesn't count?"

"Juan is my friend!"

"Uh-huh."

"He is."

"He's adorable, Rob, and he loves you."

"He does not love me."

"Yes, he does. I can tell. You need to ask him out."

"No way."

"Why not?"

"Because he'll say no." He stood. "You see this?" He massaged his stomach. "This is too flabby."

"So?"

"So he'll say no. He's a little guy. Very toned. No way he would go for me."

"You're saying he'll turn you down because you're not in perfect shape?"

"Yes. These younger guys, it's all about physicality."

"Juan is not like that. And I know he likes you. I can tell by the way he is around you. He's in love."

"Madness, please. You've lost your mind."

She took another sip as he sat. "Rob, you're the one who's mad. Not everyone is into absolute perfection. I know I'm not."

"You're not a man, and yes, you are into perfection. Look at this place."

"I have taste, Rob. There's a difference."

"It looks like a gay wet dream in here."

"I get my ideas from home décor catalogues, so what?"

"It's spotless."

"Is not. There are morning dishes in the sink and my bed is unmade."

"What else?"

She had to think a moment. "I probably left my robe and towel on the floor in the bathroom."

"Oh, bad girl." He laughed.

"I don't have kids, and other than my wine, I have no vices. So I prefer to decorate and to tidy up. What's wrong with that?"

"Well, for starters, it's all you do. And for…whatever comes after starters, you don't have anyone to share it with. Who sees this big beautiful home other than Marv and me?"

She sipped more wine, considering how to answer. She decided to be coy. "My home is decorated in a Southwestern theme. Lots of homes are. It's nothing special. As for who sees it, whoever walks in is welcome."

Rob grimaced at her and helped himself to more chocolate. After several moments of silence she was satisfied he'd given up.

"How's the team?" she asked, referring to his rugby team. He'd been playing and coaching rugby for years. His gay men's team was number one in their region.

"Good."

"Juan's playing well despite his size?" She couldn't help but smile in bringing Juan up again.

"Yes. And your point is?"

"Ask him out."

"What about you, missy? You ask someone out." Damn it, he'd turned the tide again.

"I don't have anyone to ask out." There.

"We will have to find someone, then."

"No." Where was this headed?

"Yes," he said.

"Bad idea. Let's drop it. I promise I won't bring up Juan anymore."

"Oh, no. We're going with this one. I will find someone and we will double date."

"You'll ask Juan?"

"Yes."

"Okay, then. This might be worth it." She grinned.

"You can't refuse the woman, though. You have to promise to sit through the entire date and be polite and engaging."

She groaned. "Fine."

He set down his glass and thrust out his hand. "Shake on it."

She did and laughed. "You're crazy."

"Crazy like a fox."

"Please tell me you'll find someone with half a brain this time."

"No promises. Besides, if she's cute and into you, you could have a great night."

"You know I'm not into one-night stands."

"What about weekend stands?"

"No."

"You need to live a little. You'll never meet anyone if you stay holed away in here, listening to jazz and drowning in your bottles."

"Maybe I don't want to."

"Seriously?" His face clouded. "Madness, you are wonderful. Too wonderful to spend life alone."

"I'm happy."

"You're secure."

"Don't give me the psychological mumbo jumbo I know you so badly want to."

"Don't worry, I know better than to engage any with you." He blinked and said, "Kisses."

At one time he and Madison had worked together in the counseling field. They'd had their own practice counseling youth, and things had gone quite well. But both had yearned for more and they had quickly burned out with the way young kids were being parented, not to mention the red tape and turns of cheeks within the system. So they'd decided to make a change. Rob had moved on to veterinarian school while she invested in her ranch. They were both, she was happy to say, doing well.

She was helping kids, more so than ever, and Rob was too, coaching his young rugby teams. Many of the boys that had come through the ranch had ended up playing for Rob. They still needed the intense physical work, and Rob used their energy and tenacity on the field. It was the perfect match.

Rob downed the rest of his wine and sat quietly for several moments. She thought about offering him more, but she knew he would fall asleep on her. Mondays were early morning rugby practices and Rob was usually out like a light the second he sat still. His eyes started to drift closed as Flaca came in and settled at his feet. Beamer and Lila were no doubt out on their evening prowl around the property.

"Rob?"

One eye opened to look at her.

"I know, I know. Next time I'm bringing jammies so we can listen to jazz and I can drink myself to sleep." He said the same thing at least twice a week. He stood and stretched.

"Go get some rest."

"Can't. The boys have a practice tonight. I gotta get going."

"Another one?"

"The young team."

She tossed him a piece of chocolate as she stood. "One for the road."

"You're evil. Oh, and God, how I wish I could take a glass with me. That wine is divine with this chocolate."

"You can." She crossed to the kitchen, corked the bottle, and handed it over.

"No." He pushed it away. "I couldn't. You've given me, like, three bottles this month."

"Take it."

"No. You save it for your date."

"I'm not bringing a date back here." She laughed at his confidence. There was no way he'd find a woman she'd even consider a second date with, much less a one-night stand of hot, steamy, passionate, wet sex. *Whoa, where did that come from?* She turned away, confused by the runnings of her mind.

"Well, whatever. You keep it, okay?" His voice grew soft as if he knew something was wrong. "Maybe the four of us could share it. You never know."

"Yeah," she said forcing a small smile. "You never know."

He watched her closely, then enveloped her into a quick, tight hug. "Firm embrace," he said, just like always.

"Firm embrace," she repeated.

He stepped out into the mudroom and into his shoes. Flaca followed him out to his truck, gave his hand her customary good-bye lick, and then came back to the house as he drove away. Madison watched his dirt trail and gave Marv a wave as he too left for the night. The ranch was hers alone now as the new blue of twilight darkened in the sky. She shed her slippers, walked the hall to her bedroom, and stripped. Her towel and robe were hung neatly in their place and she smiled, knowing Rob probably knew that too. He never bought her bullshit. Not totally.

She got the shower good and hot and stepped in to lather herself. The dirty water ringed the drain at her feet, and oftentimes she liked to stand and watch it until it ran clear. In the summer it seemed to take longer. Tonight it didn't take too long, but she still washed twice and hung her head to let the water knead her neck. When she was finished, she felt pliable, like her skin would be easy to maneuver if someone should try. It was a feeling that went hand in hand with her records and her wine. Pliability. To be easily moved and maneuvered. She slid into her satin robe and returned to the larger sitting area. With her remotes, new bottle of wine, and the dogs, who had come while she showered, she settled in, turned on the fireplace, and started up the stereo. She chose her favorite playlist and eased back into the oversized chaise lounge. And as Coltrane and Ellington began to play, she drank her 2005 Bergstrom Pinot Noir and willed her mind not to think of Grace Hollings.

CHAPTER SEVEN

"Jake. Jake, get up." Grace stood in the doorway with her robe hanging loosely despite being tied. Her hair was wet from her shower and she hoped like hell she wouldn't have to battle Jake this morning. She was running late. Again.

Jake mumbled and rolled over. He forced himself up and wiped the drool from his face. His hair stuck up on one side and he looked like he'd slept as hard as she'd suspected. "What time is it?"

"Time to get up."

He stood and stretched. "God, I'm sore."

"A nice hot shower will help. Hurry up, though, we don't have much time."

He trudged to the bathroom and slammed the door. Grace hurried to her room and finished getting ready. When she emerged, Jake was pouring himself a huge bowl of Frosted Flakes.

"I don't want to go today," he said.

"Yeah, me neither."

"No, seriously. I'm not going."

She sighed and stopped in front of the refrigerator. "Jake, not this morning. Please."

"It sucks there."

"You have to go."

"No, I don't."

"We've been through this."

"Yeah, well, I'm leaving. Right after I eat."

She poured herself a glass of orange juice. "What about your ankle monitor?"

"I'll cut it off."

"They will know. As soon as you try."

He paused, spoon nearly to his mouth. "Bullshit."

"Really."

He lowered his spoon and she spoke.

"Look, Jake, I know the place isn't great. But it beats juvie and it isn't forever. Besides, you get to work with that baby horse. Ms. Clark said so herself."

"Yeah, after I slave away all day. No thanks."

"Well, you have no choice. So come on. We're already running late."

"But I'm eating and I didn't get to play video games at all last night."

"Bring your cereal with you and you can play tonight."

"Damn it, Aunt Grace." He stood and cupped his bowl.

"Stop talking to me like that."

"You're making me late."

"I thought you didn't care?"

"I don't."

"Then get in the car and quit complaining."

She returned the orange juice and grabbed his water cooler, which she'd filled and chilled the night before.

They drove in silence with the occasional sound of Jake slurping his cereal. Panic settled in over both of them when she missed the correct turnoff for the ranch.

"I'm gonna be late!"

"I'm trying, Jake." She checked her mirrors and did a U-turn. They got stopped at a light.

"She's gonna make me run." He fidgeted in his seat and ran nervous hands over his new jeans. "I'm gonna be running for the rest of my life. It's all your fault, Aunt Grace."

"Calm down." But she was panicking too and she gunned the engine and drove back to the proper turnoff. Dirt flew up behind them as she continued onto the dirt road. Jake began to sway back and forth. She'd never seen him so worried or concerned before.

"She's gonna make me run. I'm gonna get the shit chores."

"I'm going as fast as I can."

"Then go faster!" He whipped his damp hair behind his ears and snugged on his ball cap. "This is a joke, Aunt Grace."

She looked at him in shock and they hit a hole. The car jolted a little but she caught control.

"Jesus Christ!" Jake shouted. "You're gonna kill us."

She yelled back. "I'm doing the best I can, Jake!"

"Well, maybe your best isn't good enough!"

"I—" But the words penetrated and they bit into her conscience. She floored the Mercedes as she turned at the ranch sign, forcing the vehicles leaving to pull off to the side.

"Hurry, Aunt Grace, hurry! It's six forty-seven!"

"Jake, shut up, please just shut up! I can't go any faster."

She saw Madison Clark directly ahead, clipboard in hand, scowl on her face. Grace slammed on the brakes as three dogs came at her from the front and sides. The car halted fiercely, jerking her and Jake in their seat belts. Dust shrouded them and the dogs yipped outside the vehicle. Jake was out of the car and scrambling toward Madison before Grace could put the car in park. She saw him run up to her, throw up his hands, and then bow his head as she spoke.

"Shit." Grace crawled from the car and walked carefully in her plum-colored high heels and matching suit. She shooed the dogs that enclosed her, still yipping. They stopped once she reached Jake and Madison.

"Tell her, Aunt Grace. Tell her it's your fault," Jake pleaded breathlessly.

"It is. I'm terribly sorry. Please don't punish him for it. I woke up late and—"

Madison blinked but said nothing. Then she looked at her clipboard. "You're three minutes late, Jake. Get started on those laps."

"But—"

"Yes, ma'am?"

He closed his mouth, gave Grace a deadly look, and took off.

Madison watched him for a moment. "The run'll do him good. Get rid of that anger. It's too early for that kind of anger."

"In my opinion he has a right to be angry. It's my fault we're late. I woke up late and I had to get Jake going—"

"Jake doesn't have an alarm clock?"

Grace stammered. "Uh, yes, but…"

"But what?"

She stopped and stared at her. She was every bit the same stern cowgirl she was before. Only her jeans were worn and faded and fit loosely. A thick brown leather belt held them up on her trim waist, with a faded navy T-shirt tucked haphazardly in on one side. She was a lesbian's dream, but Grace only tasted the acid the woman brought up in her.

"Look, I'm sorry he's late."

"Don't apologize to me," she said as she eyed Jake, who was running and breathing hard, his face already red.

"I—"

"Yes?"

"Nothing." Grace turned, walked carefully to her car, and brought out his water cooler. She set it on the ground along with the $3.50 for lunch. "It won't happen again."

"Let's hope not." She eyed Grace quickly, sweeping her gaze up and down her body. Then she tugged on her hat. "Have a nice day."

Grace remained still, wondering about the look. Was it interest? Or contempt? Did it matter?

She waved to Jake and turned to leave. The white dog followed her, touching a cold nose to her leg. Grace climbed in the car and was disappointed to find that Madison had moved toward the stables.

"Did I want her to watch me or what?"

She started the car and backed out. The dog chased her all the way down the dirt road.

CHAPTER EIGHT

"It wasn't my fault," Jake said as he stumbled up to Madison and bent. He coughed and spat and sucked in hurried breaths.

"Stand straight and breathe deeply. It helps." Madison was brushing down Draco, her blackest and wildest gelding.

Jake hesitated but then did as instructed. He even raised his arms. "Aunt Grace, she woke up so late I hardly had time to eat. I had to eat my cereal in the car."

"I suppose you want me to pity you, then? Feel badly?"

He looked appalled. "Well, just know it wasn't my fault."

"I think some of it was."

"What?"

He reached up and tried to pet Draco, but the gelding turned his head.

"You need to be responsible for you, Jake. As a young man."

"But I—"

"That means setting your own alarm, making sure you have the proper clothes ready, making your own lunch, and getting your own water. You don't need to wait for your aunt."

"She always wakes me up."

"But she's late. So take responsibility for yourself and take care of it. Do it all yourself. You're well old enough."

"What if she's still late?"

"Wake her up. Help her out."

He crossed his arms. "I shouldn't have to."

"She shouldn't have to do those things for you either, but she does. She does it because she loves you."

"She does not. I'm just a burden. A thorn in her ass."

"I'm not going to pity you, Jake. And you owe me a lap for cursing."

He stomped his foot and stifled another curse.

"Do yourself a favor, Jake. Do the things I told you to do. Get up on your own and get ready. It will help your aunt out, and if she's late again we'll talk, okay?"

"Yeah."

"What?"

"Yes, ma'am."

"Go do that lap and then help Michael."

"I gotta do the shit chores again?"

"That's another lap."

He sauntered off, mumbling.

Madison fit a bit into Draco's mouth and harnessed him with a rein. He fought at first like he always did but eventually calmed enough to be led from the stables. The sun was starting to shine brightly as she walked him into the main pen. Two of her more seasoned boys were waiting, watching her closely. Marv was also there, leaning on the rails.

"He's a real looker, that wild one."

"Yes, he is," Madison said. "Too bad he's not well behaved." She stopped with the horse in the middle of the pen. "Okay, boys, watch closely. We're going to continue working with Draco today. I'm going to run him for a little while and then one of you can." In the distance she saw Jake approach, sweat covering his face. He'd just finished running and was interested in watching. She couldn't afford to give him that luxury, though.

"Marv, will you show Jake where Michael is?"

"Sure thing."

"Can't I watch? Just for a little while?"

"Not now, Jake. You've got chores."

"Why aren't they doing their chores?"

Draco pulled away from his loud voice, and she calmed him.

"First of all, Jake, I don't have to answer to you. Secondly, these boys did their morning chores while you were busy running. Thirdly, they've earned the right and learned the ability to be able to work with this horse. One day you may too. But you better start with minding me and doing your chores without whining and questioning."

"Come on, Jake." Marv led him away, but not before Madison caught the angry and embarrassed look on his face. The boy was going to be hard to break. More so than Draco.

She ticked at Draco and got him started. She first led him into a walk around her and then eventually into a trot. She checked out his form, his muscles, and his movements. He looked gorgeous with the sun shining off his inky skin. He truly was a beautiful horse. But then he started fighting her, tugging a little here and there. Once she had him straightened out again, she stopped and called in the boys. One at a time she let them try, with her right there next to them. Two weeks ago it would've been impossible, but Draco had come along well with his training. He allowed both boys to run him for about a minute before he started acting up, at which point she took the rope. She ran him some more, instructing the boys and talking to Draco, ticking at him and giving him praise. When she finished she allowed the boys to help again, this time simply walking him around the pen. He'd worked up a good sweat and he needed calming and cooling down. Then she'd let the boys brush him and feed him and allow him to graze for a while. It was good therapy for both Draco and the boys. Horses had a way with people. A way she couldn't quite explain with words. It was the same with dogs. Hers rose as she headed to the side porch for some water. They followed with the exception of Lila, who stayed near the stables, keeping everyone in her sight.

Madison settled in for some water from the big serving cooler. She went over Jake's file in her mind. There wasn't much she didn't already know, and most of his criminal record wasn't on hand. But the judge had provided her with enough to work with. He had been neglected by his mother, who was addicted to drugs. His aunt had intervened and gained temporary custody about six months ago. Truancy was his main issue, along with a brief scuffle with the law.

Grace Hollings was an attorney, and a good one, based on the website she'd checked out. She was also in way over her head with Jake, and Madison was finding it more and more difficult not to talk to her about it. She could see her sinking and wondered how much she did indeed care. How hard was it to get up a little bit earlier to make sure Jake got here on time? Did she think her excuses would get him off? She made a note to talk to her about it again this evening. She'd seen this behavior in other parents, but from Grace it annoyed her more. Was it because she was beautiful? Or because she was so self-righteous?

Her beauty did have its advantages. Madison had caught herself looking today and she was still upset over it. But the dark purple suit with the gray blouse had really set off Grace's hair and skin, and Madison wanted to drink her like a tall glass of water and just stare at her for a long, long while, looking at those long, long legs in those heels, wondering what was underneath the suit—

She shook her from her mind and looked over her clipboard. So far they were set for the week. No new horses and no new kids. At least not so far. But calls came in at all hours when it came to the horses. And new boys were always being sentenced, either by their parents or the courts. She preferred to start them on Mondays but had made exceptions before.

A loud horse whinny startled her from her seat. She flew to the edge of the deck as it continued, followed by shouts and galloping chaos. She jumped the deck and headed for the main pen looking for the boys and Draco. But neither was there. She followed a huge mass of floating dust to where three of them stood along with Marv.

"He's gone off on Draco!" Marv said.

"Who?"

"Jake!"

Marv ran to give chase as she caught sight of boy and horse rounding the stables. "Oh God." Jake was bouncing, barely hanging on, and Draco started to buck. She took off at a sprint just as Jake was thrown from the horse. Draco continued on at a mad bucking, wild pace, but at least he cleared the boy. She shouted at Bobby as he ran out from the stables, arms and hands wet from bathing Mazey. "Go get Draco! He's loose."

Marv reached Jake first and when she came up on them, she knelt and told him not to move.

"His arm," Marv said. "Says it's broke."

"Jake? Jake, can you talk to me?" She heard him sobbing. "Jake, are you all right?"

"No."

"What hurts?"

"My arm."

"Anything else?"

"I don't know. My wrist is killing me."

"Does your back hurt? Your neck?"

"No."

"Well, lie still. I need to get EMS out here."

"What? No!"

He rolled over and stood despite Marv trying to hold him down. "You call the hospital and I'll run off right now."

He held his wrist in his right hand, tears streaking his dirty face.

"Jake, we have to call. And we have to call your aunt too." She nodded at Marv, who moved away to make the call. "But don't worry about that. Come on. Let's get in the shade over on the patio." The other boys caught up, curious and frightened.

"He's okay. He's okay." She placed a hand on his shoulder and led him across the ranch. The boys followed along with the dogs. Lila was panting, having chased Draco and Jake as they rounded the stables. Madison scratched her head and eased Jake down into a chair. His body shook and his brow was bleeding. The rest of him looked to be intact. Filthy but intact.

"Man, that was crazy," one of the boys said.

"Yeah, killer crazy. The way you took off on him. No saddle or nothing!"

Madison turned with a stern look. "Go on back to your duties."

"Yes, ma'am." They walked away slowly, some slapping their

hats on their thighs. She saw Bobby round the corner with another staff member. They had Draco in tow and were checking him over for injury. He seemed to be okay, but he needed to walk and calm down. She was glad to see Bobby take him back to the pen to do just that.

She pulled a chair up next to Jake and touched his shoulder. He was still trembling, but he jerked nevertheless.

"Jake?" She turned his chin. "Jake, look at me." She was speaking softly. "Tell me how you are. Does your head hurt?"

"No." But then he flinched when he touched his brow. "I don't know."

"Can I ask you something?"

He turned away. "You're gonna yell at me. Or make me run. Well, I can't run."

She shook her head and laughed softly. This caused him to turn back. "You mean you're not mad?" he said.

"No, I'm not mad." She'd had boys cause more ruckus than this little episode. She just hoped Jake and Draco would be okay.

"How come?"

"I was scared, Jake. Scared for you, scared for my horse. Looks like you took the worst of it, though."

"That makes you happy? That I got hurt and he didn't?"

Whoa. This kid really felt unloved and unworthy.

"No. I'm glad you're both relatively okay. Even though you're the one who chose to do this. Draco sure didn't." She couldn't let him off the hook.

He licked his lips and stared at his boots. "What did you want to ask?"

She sat back and crossed her legs. "Why did you do it?"

He breathed deeply and she was relieved to see that he didn't seem to have any rib pain. She also didn't notice any knots on his head. His arm, best she could make out, was either sprained or fractured. There were no cuts or protrusions. Just the one on his brow. It would need a butterfly bandage or a few stitches, but so far he didn't seem seriously injured.

"I got upset."

"Why?"

"Because I had to run, like, five freaking miles and then I had to clean up shit. It isn't fair!"

"It is fair, Jake. Those are the rules. Dozens of boys just like you have had to follow them and they didn't like it either at first. But the rules are there for a reason. They keep us safe and they keep us responsible."

He didn't seem to like her answer.

"You see Bobby over there?"

He nodded while playing with his sore wrist.

"He came here about six years ago. Court ordered, just like you."

"Really?" He studied him.

"Yes, and let me tell you, he hated it here. With a capital *H*. I won't tell you all he did, but he wasn't a fan of the rules and he ran so much he lost ten pounds in two weeks."

"What happened? I mean, why is he here now?"

"Because he grew to love it. We got Mazey when he was here and he just fell in love with her and she with him. They helped each other heal and he never looked back. He graduated from high school and came to me and asked if he could volunteer. He did so well I took him on."

"I don't think I'm going to love it."

She laughed again. "Never say never, Jake. Not around here."

"Have other boys loved it? I mean, I know your two favorites do."

"My favorites?"

"The ones with Draco."

"They earned that spot, Jake. The work you've done? Multiply it by twenty and add about four more miles."

"You don't like them better?"

"No. I don't have favorites. I have workers. I have boys who need help. I have horses who need help too. Mix it all together and that's what I focus on. When the boys listen and help and do as they are told, I appreciate it. They get to spend more one-on-one time with the horses, which benefits the both of them."

"How can a horse help me?" He flinched as he moved his arm.

"You wait and see."

"What about Draco?"

"What about him?"

"Can I work with him?"

"Maybe."

"He's cool. I like him."

"What about that colt?"

He shrugged. "He's okay. He's cute."

"Marv thinks you did well with him."

"I didn't do anything special."

"Someone say my name?" Marv asked as he stepped out of the house. He touched Madison on the shoulder. "EMS should be here soon. His aunt's on her way. She didn't sound too happy."

"By the time she gets here he'll be gone."

"I told you I'm not going to any hospital!" He tried to stand, but Marv helped him remain with a gentle push on his shoulders.

"There, there. No one said anything about a hospital, okay?" he said, giving Madison a concerned look.

"You may need stitches, Jake. And that arm needs an x-ray."

"I said no! I just want Aunt Grace to get here." He dissolved into sudden tears.

"She said she's not too far out. Was out meeting witnesses or clients or something."

Madison rose and covered him with a light blanket. She too touched his shoulder. He jerked, but only from his desperate-sounding sobs. Why didn't this kid want to go to a hospital? She leaned forward and placed her hand over his. He continued to cry for a few more minutes, eventually moving his hand away and quieting. Around them, the ranch carried on. Birds sang, boys called out, and horses grazed in the pens. Jake watched through watery eyes until eventually Marv pointed.

"Here comes EMS," he said, looking beyond her. Madison followed his line of sight and saw the ambulance working its way up the trail, lights on with no sound. Jake stood and began to pace.

"I'm not going. I'm not going."

"Jake, just let them take a look at you, okay?" She had to calm him down. He looked to be in fight-or-flight mode and he was in no condition to do either.

"They're gonna take me. They're gonna take me without Aunt Grace and she'll never find me. She'll never find me!"

"Jake, Jake, shh, it's okay." She tried to touch him again, but he slinked away from her.

Marv's face fell as he met Madison's eyes. Something was wrong, and they both felt helpless.

"Jake, we won't let them take you anywhere until your aunt gets here," he said.

Jake turned on him quickly with wild, desperate eyes. He reminded Madison so much of Grace it nearly took her breath away. The doe eyes, the shimmering light hair. And that look…so intense and seeking. She cleared her tight throat and agreed. "That's right. We'll just let them look at you. No one goes anywhere until your aunt gets here."

"You're lying," he said.

Marv held up his hands. "We don't lie."

"It's a rule, remember?" Madison reminded him.

Jake looked to the patio floor, then back up. "Swear?"

"On my daddy," Marv said. "Here, we'll shake on it." He held out his right hand and Jake released his injured arm to shake limply.

The ambulance tires cracked on the gravel drive, coming to a stop very close to them. Jake's shoulders fell as if in defeat. He looked like a hunched, blanketed bag of bones. Helpless. It tugged at Madison's heart despite his attitude of indifference and defiance. The boy was hurting, inside and out, and it was plainly obvious now.

"This our guy?" a man asked, crawling from the vehicle. A built woman followed, immediately homing in on Madison.

"Yes, sir," Marv said. "This is Jake."

"Hey there, Jake," the man said, snapping on gloves as he entered the patio. "I hear you took a spill off a horse."

Jake nodded but refused to meet his gaze.

"Will you come sit over here for me?"

The woman came as well and carefully removed his blanket. She was thick with muscle and had short, curly brown hair. Her skin and face had seen the sun for many years.

Madison assumed she was gay just by the looks the woman kept giving her. Brief glances here and there to size her up, a small smile. She wasn't unattractive but she wasn't Madison's type. She was, however, very good with Jake, taking his vitals and asking him questions. Both examined him completely and he yelped when they looked at his arm. And when they mentioned taking a ride to the hospital for x-rays and a CT scan of his head, he bolted upward again.

Madison had to explain. "We're waiting on his aunt for that decision."

"Where is she?" the woman asked, looking to Madison.

"She's on her way."

"We can't wait too long," the man said.

"Can you bandage up that brow and splint his arm in the meantime?"

The woman smiled. "Sure. Ms.?"

"Clark."

"Sure thing, Ms. Clark."

They retrieved supplies from the back of the ambulance and set to work on Jake. As they were splinting his arm, Madison heard the sound of the Mercedes engine gunning. Tires kicked and spat and Grace flew onto the drive like a stunt driver. All heads turned to look as she climbed from the car and tried her best to run in her heels toward the patio.

"What the hell happened?" she demanded, whipping off her sunglasses. "What the hell was he doing on a wild horse?" She glared at Madison and scurried quickly to Jake. "You're supposed to take care of him!" She held his face. "Oh my God, oh my God. You're bleeding and—" She saw his arm. "Is your arm broken?" She turned to Marv. "You said he wasn't seriously hurt! Just what the hell kind of show are you running here?" The question was aimed at Madison, who burned with anger. It was understandable for Grace to be upset, but to place blame right away without knowing the whole story? Madison fought remarking in return and instead clenched her jaw tightly shut.

"We don't think he's seriously hurt," said the female EMT, seeming to pick up on the tension. "We just want to take him in to be sure. He probably needs some stitches and he needs his arm and head looked at just to be safe."

"Stitches? His arm and head? Sounds pretty damn serious to me."

"Standard procedure with this type of fall."

"I'm sorry. Who are you?"

"Wy."

"Wy?"

"As in Wynona."

"Oh, well, thank you, Wy, but I'll take it from here."

"You're going to take him in yourself?"

"Please, Aunt Grace, no. I don't want to go."

"Yes, I'll handle it."

He began to tremble again.

"Shh, shh. We'll talk about it."

"We're going to need you to sign something, then. I'll get the papers while Henry bandages up that wound." Wy headed back to the ambulance.

"You really should take him in," Marv said softly.

"You think?" Grace shot back. "Thank you very much, but I know how to care for my nephew."

"No, Aunt Grace. Don't make me go."

"Baby, you have to." She squeezed his uninjured arm. "I'll be right there with you, I promise."

"You won't leave my side?"

"No, of course not."

"Not even for a second?"

"No."

"And I won't get lost? And they won't do to me what they did to Mom?"

Grace fell to her knees. “No, they won’t.”

“Actually, if they take him for x-rays and scans, you probably won’t be able to go in with him,” Henry said somberly.

Grace glared and Jake started up again. “Aunt Grace!”

“She can go with him,” Madison said, stepping forward. “I’ll call ahead and make sure.” She had a connection or two at the local hospital. She’d make sure he was well cared for, along with Grace. It was the least she could do to make sure he actually went to get examined.

Jake grew quiet and whispered something to Grace. Marv shifted and eyed Madison as if he’d heard.

“No. Out of the question,” Grace said.

“Then I don’t want to go!”

“Jake, stop this. You’re going. I will take you and I won’t leave you.”

“I want her to come too. Ms. Clark.”

“Well, she can’t.”

“Why not?”

“Why do you want her to go?”

“Because she—I trust her.”

Grace went slack as if the wind had been knocked from her.

“I won’t go without you and her both.”

Madison wanted to walk away. She was feeling so many things from anger to confusion to worry about imposing. She’d been by her boys’ sides before with injuries, but it was obvious Grace didn’t want her around. This felt more like a family issue, and Jake was not hers.

“That’s it for us, then,” Henry said, putting away his gear.

“If you’ll just sign here.” Wy handed a clipboard to Grace, who signed quickly. Then Wy approached Madison and spoke softly.

“If you want I can call ahead too. Let the ER know you’re coming. I know some of the nurses.”

“Excuse me,” Grace said rising. “If you’re talking about my nephew, I’d prefer it if you speak to me.”

“I was just offering to call ahead to some of the nurses I know.”

"That won't be necessary."

"Okay, then." She shrugged and slipped Madison a business card. "Just in case." She smiled apologetically. "Or if you need anything else. My cell's on there." She nodded at Grace and followed Henry to the ambulance. They climbed in and drove away slowly.

Jake stood and walked surprisingly fast directly up to Madison. "Please come with me. I'll feel safer."

"Jake," Grace said. "Jake, don't put her in this position."

"Please, Ms. Clark. I know you won't let them hurt me."

"I can't promise that, Jake," she whispered, wishing she could.

"See?" he said to Grace. "She's real with me. I trust her. With both of you there I'll feel better. Please, Ms. Clark."

Tears welled in his eyes. Those familiar brown eyes. Two pairs boring down on Madison.

She sighed and looked to Marv. He nodded once and headed back toward the stables.

"Okay."

Grace nervously tucked loose strands of her hair behind her ears.

Jake tried not to sob. "Thank you."

"We'd better get going," Madison said. She cleared her throat again, trying not to let the boy's emotion get to her. He was more vulnerable and sensitive than she'd ever considered, and his tears and pleas had tugged on her heart. "I'll follow you."

She rounded the house to her own private drive and climbed up into her dually truck. The keys were always in the visor so she caught them in midair and started the engine. By the time she backed out and reached the driveway, the Mercedes was well ahead of her, kicking up dirt as usual.

"What am I doing?" she asked, shaking her head. "What am I doing?"

CHAPTER NINE

"Aunt Grace, don't leave!" Jake shouted from the hospital bed in the busy ER. A doctor had just examined him and they were waiting to send him to get his head and arm scanned. A nurse was tucking pillows in behind him and adjusting the TV remote for his good hand.

"I'm not, honey. I'm just going behind this curtain to talk to Ms. Clark. We'll be right here." She motioned for Madison to follow, then yanked the curtain closed behind them just before she started in. "Just what the hell happened? Why weren't you watching him? Why—"

"Don't speak to me like that," Madison whispered, anger on her face.

"I'm sorry. How should I speak to you now that my nephew is laid up in a hospital bed from a fall at *your* ranch? Should I be polite? Do I not have enough manners for you?" She was so sick of the high-and-mighty attitude of Madison Clark.

"Frankly, no, you don't. You've been rude from day one. Inconsiderate of the rules—"

"Rude? Excuse me? You're the one who's been rude." What was with this woman? Grace was so mad she could just haul off and hit something. She considered screaming into the pillow of the empty bed next to them and pummeling it into nonexistence.

"Enough," Madison said.

"No, it's not enough. Tell me what the hell happened to my nephew!" She had to lower her voice, praying Jake couldn't hear.

"Why don't you ask him?"

"I did."

"And what did he say?"

"That he tried to ride a horse on his own."

Madison pulled the curtain open and stood next to Jake. "Tell your aunt what happened today."

He hesitated. "I did."

"All of it."

"I—"

"Remember the rule about lying."

He closed his eyes. "Fine."

The nurse left them, and Madison fingered down the volume on the TV remote. Grace grew nervous, not liking the look on either one's face.

"I had to do shit chores again today, and Ms. Clark wouldn't let me work with this cool horse named Draco."

"Tell it without the cursing."

"He's on my time now," Grace interrupted. "Jake, no cursing." She blushed at how ridiculous she'd just sounded.

"So I got tired of shoveling sh—uh, crap and I threw down my shovel and took off. I saw the horse, grabbed the reins, stood on the fence, and climbed on." He smiled. "I rode him a good ways too."

"Before he bucked you off," Madison said, crossing her arms, obviously displeased.

"And where were you when this happened?" Grace asked Madison.

"On my patio doing paperwork."

"Paperwork?"

Madison crossed back behind the curtain, jerked her head at Grace to follow, and then pulled the curtain closed.

"Do not question me like that in front of him. It brings my authority into question."

"That's exactly what it's meant to do."

"Look, Jake was assigned to a chore with another boy. Two staff members were in the stable with them. When he took off, he took off at a run. The whole thing was over in less than two minutes. No one could've stopped him or foreseen what he was going to do. When we did, my staff and I reacted right away. He's lucky he's okay."

"You're damn right he is." How could she stand there so calmly and relay this story, as if none of it was her fault? Jake was hurt! Terrified and shaken. "He won't be coming back to the ranch."

Madison stared at her for a long moment. Then she removed her cowboy hat to reveal the sweat-coated blue bandana wrapped around her head. Grace could smell dirt, sweat, and suntan lotion. Strangely, it stirred her. She forced herself to look away from the intense stormy eyes and sun-kissed sharp cheekbones.

"I just don't think it's the best place for Jake," Grace said.

Madison sank onto the empty bed behind her. "It is the best place. And this event should prove that to you."

"Him getting hurt? Are you insane?" She had to look away again. Madison was sitting there with her elbows on her knees and hat in hands. She looked so handsome and hard-worked. And beautifully…butch.

"He got hurt because he didn't follow the rules. He doesn't like the ranch because he doesn't follow the rules."

"Rules. That's all you talk about."

"Perhaps that's what you need more of."

"Excuse me? Don't tell me how to raise my nephew."

"I'm not. I merely suggested."

"Aunt Grace?"

They came out from behind the curtain to see a worker wearing scrubs maneuvering the bed to roll away. "Time for his CT scan," he said with a smile.

"Aunt Grace, no. Tell them you have to come." He began to panic and the color drained from his face.

"I need to go with him," she said.

"You can't go in the room with him. I'm sorry."

Jake began to wail and breathe heavily. Madison went to his side and took his uninjured hand. She looked at the worker. "We are going with him. As far as we can." When the worker didn't respond, Madison took him by the elbow to the door. "Otherwise this will continue and you will have to sedate a thirteen-year-old boy."

"Okay, okay." He nodded quickly.

"Jake, I'm coming with you," Grace said, trying to get him to stop. "Shh, I'm right here." She patted his hand. "I'm coming. See?" She walked next to the bed as the worker pushed it down the hall.

"I want Ms. Clark. Ms. Clark too."

"She's waiting for us in the room."

"No! Ms. Clark!" he called out. "Ms. Clark!"

Madison came out of the room and hurried to his side. "Jake, you need to calm down." She looked at Grace with obvious questions in her eyes.

"Don't leave me. Don't leave me."

"I'm not."

"I'm here, Jake," Grace added and he finally calmed with her on one side and Madison on the other. They entered a room where two other workers looked at them with surprise. The one pushing shook his head as if to say *don't ask*. Grace helped Jake move onto the small sliding bench. Madison too came to his side.

"Jake, I know how these things work. First of all, it doesn't touch you. Secondly, you just lie still and your aunt and I will be behind the window. We aren't leaving you. We will be right here."

Grace was amazed when he didn't argue. The workers nodded in agreement and gave him further instructions.

"You swear you won't leave?" he asked Madison.

Grace took his hand. "I swear."

"I want her to say it."

The demand stung, but Grace would do and take whatever was necessary for him to get the scan done.

"I swear," Madison said.

"Okay," he breathed. "Okay."

They moved into a control room and Grace waved at him through the window. He looked so small and fragile lying there on the sliding bench. She saw his good hand clench as the workers eased him into the hole of the machine. He lay very still as the procedure was carried out and his head scanned. She held her breath, afraid he would move. Madison broke the silence.

"Why is he so afraid?"

"He—" Grace glanced at her and looked away; Madison's eyes were too penetrating. "When he was five he was taken to the hospital with his mother, who had apparently overdosed on something. He was left next to her on the hospital floor and when he wandered off to get help, they were separated. From a distance, he saw the doctors begin CPR and stab a needle into her. He was convinced they had killed her. He hid in room after room in the middle of the night with sick and dying people. When nurses saw him they tried to help, but he just kept running. When they finally caught him he was nearly catatonic with shock and exhaustion. To make matters worse, he was then brought to his mother to identify her and she was unconscious, hooked up to machines. It only terrified him more. He's never gone near a hospital since."

"That explains a lot," Madison whispered.

"Yes."

"He's been through a lot, hasn't he?"

This time Grace met her eyes. "More than you can imagine."

"I'm sorry," she said.

"For what?"

"For him."

Grace pressed her lips together and nodded. He'd been through too much, and she felt so damned responsible for not knowing most of it until recently.

"And for you."

"Me?"

"Yes."

Grace saw the sincerity in her eyes and her heart warmed so profusely she thought her lungs would melt in sheer bliss. "Don't be," she whispered. "I love him, through thick and thin, and I'd do anything for him."

"Then let him keep coming to the ranch."

"I—" But she didn't know what to say. The day's events had traumatized both her and Jake. She needed time to think.

The CT scan was finished, and they walked alongside Jake's gurney to the x-ray room. Madison didn't say anything else, and Grace was relieved. She couldn't yet make a decision, and she wasn't about to make one when her body was overreacting to a little kindness. It didn't help matters when they returned to the ER and Madison held Jake's hand as his brow was stitched up. She told him calm stories of the ranch and about all the horses and what they'd persevered through. She told him about some of her former boys, and Grace found herself captivated as well, caught up in her smooth voice, her deep eyes, and the calm way in which she spoke.

Jake was so quiet and still the doctor had to ask if he was still awake when he finished.

"Yeah."

"Good job. You're all set."

They splinted his arm after confirming a sprain and gave him some pain medication for both his arm and his bruised head. All in all, he came out okay.

Grace asked to speak to Madison once again behind the curtain while a nurse tried to cheer Jake up. "I wanted to thank you for coming," she said.

Madison slipped off her bandana and sat on the bed, running her hand through her thick dirty blond layers.

"I'm glad I could help. I feel really bad about what happened." Her cheekbones were tinged red from the sun. "Had I known he was going for Draco…"

"I know," Grace said softly, trying hard not to stare at her. "You're…" Gorgeous. Strong. Caring. Beautiful. "Not responsible for what Jake did."

"Tomorrow, things will change."

Grace bit her lower lip, knowing Madison was taking it to heart. "Anyway, I just wanted to say thanks. Jake's really taken to you, and I have to admit after today…"

Madison looked up.

"After today...I thought I was going to have to kill you. But now..."

"We're okay?"

"Yes."

Madison chuckled and rose. "That's nice to hear."

"No, I mean it," Grace said, taking her arm gently. Madison stared at her hand and stood very still. "Thank you."

Madison looked into her eyes and blinked slowly. "You're welcome."

Grace released her, but only after she felt both their breathing change. Something was happening between them, and there was no denying it now.

"That woman...that EMT."

"Yes?" Madison gripped the curtain after shoving her bandana in her back pocket.

"She hit on you, didn't she?"

The flush on Madison's face was obvious and spread all the way up to her ears. "I think she was trying to help."

"Who? Jake or you?"

Madison didn't respond, just glanced away.

Grace laughed. "I thought so." She pulled the curtain open and left Madison blushing, not mentioning just how damn jealous it had made her.

"Ready to go, kiddo?"

The nurse helped by wheeling him out to the main doors. There Grace took his arm as Madison followed.

"Thank you for coming," Grace said again to Madison as they walked to their vehicles.

"You're welcome."

"Yeah, thanks," Jake said.

"Don't you have something else to say to Ms. Clark?" Grace said.

The sun was no longer bright, but it was strong enough to cause him to squint. "I guess I'm sorry," he said. "For you know, doing that."

"You guess?"

"Yeah. I mean yes, ma'am. I mean, I am sorry. I should've just done my dumb chores."

"Okay. Apology accepted. But you tacked on another day of those dumb chores."

"What? The crap chores?"

"Yes."

"Man! But I only got one arm."

"We'll work it out."

"Come on, Jake." Grace led him to the car and she watched briefly as Madison Clark walked away toward the half-hanging sun, placing her cowboy hat back on her head.

❖

A few hours later, Grace had given Jake a pain pill and helped him to bed. He had fallen asleep quickly, arm propped up on a pillow. It was nearing seven o'clock when her doorbell rang. She pulled it open quickly and smiled at Ally Murphy.

"Come in."

"He's asleep?" Ally asked.

"Yes."

"Good."

Grace led them into the living room where she offered her a glass of chardonnay. She didn't know much about wine, but it seemed appropriate. She'd had a long, tiring day and Ally probably had too. They settled on the sofa.

"So he got hurt, huh? At the ranch?"

"Yes. And I'm telling you, I just don't think it's the right place for him, Ally."

"Oh?"

"Yes."

"Why not?"

"Well, he got hurt, for God's sake."

"He could get hurt a lot worse in juvie."

"Don't they have guards in juvie?"

"Yes, but I'm not just talking physical. I'm talking mental. It's prison, Grace. The kids in there are in no way a good influence. And if he gets institutionalized, it will be all he knows and all he expects."

Grace sighed. "Well, what about this Madison Clark? Is she really the best for this sort of...instance?" Even though she was asking the question, she hoped the answer would be a positive one. There was something about Madison that made Grace want to know more.

"Madison's one of the best in the business. She knows her stuff and she's been working with troubled kids for years."

"I'm not sure what to think of her."

Ally laughed. "I didn't say she was overly friendly."

"You got that right. I mean, she wasn't at first, that's for sure." Was she now? Who knew how she'd be tomorrow or the next day.

"But she works wonders with those boys. I think she could do well with Jake too if given a chance."

"I don't know, Ally. I mean, he got hurt and she was pretty rude to me."

"Rude?"

"Yes, and at first I thought she was going to refuse to take responsibility."

"You thought she should be watching him every second?"

"Yes, don't you?"

"From what I understand, those boys are supervised just fine. It's not a place for violent offenders. Only those like Jake. And the only complaints I've heard are from parents who, you know, don't like the rules."

"Oh my God, you sound like her. So infuriating!" She stood and began to pace. "And she can be so rude and matter-of-fact and I don't know, I just think Jake needs to be better supervised."

"Such as in prison?"

"No." She sat again. "Isn't there somewhere else? Boot camp or something?"

"If Jake won't follow the rules at Healing Soul, do you really think he will at boot camp?"

"I just don't know what to do. If she wasn't so damn—"

"Right?"

"What?"

Ally set her glass on the coffee table. "Sounds like your problem is more with Madison Clark rather than anything else."

"You're—"

Ally raised a perfectly manicured eyebrow. "Jake disobeyed and ran to a horse. It wasn't saddled, no one was with it, and from what you said, the staff chased after him as quickly as they could. I think Jake got himself into a heap of trouble and they handled it pretty well. He's safe, and luckily he's okay." She stood. "If you expect Madison to do something about it, tell her. I'm sure she will anyway. Jake will most likely have to work off what he did in running or chores."

Grace felt defeated, like the air had been let out of her anger balloon. "She did. She said he would have another day of the chores he doesn't like and that things would be different tomorrow."

"Then there you go. Madison isn't a yeller or a reactive-type person. She's very stoic."

"I guess. Damn it, Ally, you're supposed to be on my side here."

She laughed. "I am. And Jake's too." She placed her glass next to Grace's.

"You think I should let him go back."

"Yes."

"And I should trust this woman."

"Yes. Now why don't you tell me the real problem, Grace?"

"Sorry?"

"Why you don't like her?"

"I'm not following."

"It's because you're attracted to her, aren't you?"

"What? No. No of course not." She stood again, flustered.

"Then why call me all the way over here, Grace? Just to complain about a strange woman? I'm not buying it."

Grace started to chew her nail but knew it looked too obviously nervous. *Why did I call her over? Why am I bitching about Madison so much when we basically made peace? Why can't I just forget her?*

That was it. She was trying to force her from her mind by being with Ally.

"You're wrong," was all she could think to say.

"Then relax, will you? And tell me why I'm here." She smiled seductively.

"I—I'm not sure."

"Well, come sit and we can figure it out."

"I think I'm just overly stressed."

"I think maybe you are. Now why don't we forget about Madison Clark for a while and you show me your bedroom?"

Grace laughed as Ally touched her face.

"I'm not sure."

"About what? Showing me your bedroom or Madison Clark?"

Both. "I told you I'm not into her."

Ally grinned and leaned in to whisper, "Then let's go in the bedroom. We'll lock the door and I'll stifle your cries with my fingers."

Grace inhaled sharply as she felt Ally's tongue tease her ear. "I don't know."

"Yes, you do. Let me do this for you, baby. Just let me."

"I don't usually—"

"Shh, don't think. Just feel. Now show me to the bedroom."

Their hands interlaced and Grace found herself leading the way. Her body hummed warmly and her mind felt numb. When she entered her room and turned, Ally closed the door, locked it, and came at her like a huntress of the night, kissing her softly but deeply. Grace fought to speak, but Ally wouldn't let her, covering her in kisses and firm caresses, undressing her in a matter of seconds. Her hand found her thighs and trailed upward where it found her center already wet and trembling.

"Oh, yes. That feels good," Ally said. "You're so ready for me."

Grace felt her eyes close and all she could think about were Ally's words.

Let's forget about Madison Clark for a while.

The phrase repeated, but she couldn't let Madison's image escape from the clutches of her mind. The way she looked when she said she was sorry, the way she held Jake's hand and insisted they go with him for the scan. She was so powerful in those moments and so roughly beautiful in others. She was a rose with thorns. A beautiful, beautiful rose just completely covered in thorns, almost impossible to see or touch.

"Lie down," Ally said, already stroking her so well she was yearning to come.

Grace considered arguing. She was the one usually in control. But her thoughts of Madison and the strokes of Ally's hand were so sweet and burningly blissful she didn't care. She just wanted to let herself go and feel nothing but erotic touch and pressure and—

"Oh," she cried as she lay back and Ally buried her head between her legs. "Oh, God." Her tongue and lips were like fire, licking her short and hard. She held her head and closed her eyes. "Oh, oh, oh."

Let's just forget about Madison Clark for a while.

When she opened her eyes again and looked down, it was Madison's head between her legs, Madison's mouth, Madison's intense eyes. And with that vision locked in her mind, she threw her herself back, dug her fingers into her sheets, and came into the night.

CHAPTER TEN

"You think he'll come?" Marv asked Madison as he held the colt between his legs and fed it from the bottle. The colt drank heartily, milk dripping from his muzzle. Madison grinned.

"I hope so."

"You hope so? You ask me, that boy's trouble. And he's spoiled. Taking off on Draco like that, I ought to tan his hide."

"There's no hide tanning."

"Too bad. It would straighten these boys out a hell of a lot quicker."

"That's debatable, and you know how I feel about it."

"Yeah, you'd rather run them to death."

She laughed. "It works. When the body struggles, the mind flourishes."

"Yeah, yeah."

"So what happened to him? Did he break his arm?"

"No, it was just a sprain, and he had to get a few stitches on that brow."

"That's good. Scared me to death when I saw him take that tumble. Thought his head was cracked for sure."

"Me too."

"Guess we're gonna have to watch him like a damn hawk. Which isn't fair to the other boys."

Madison had considered this as she sat and drank wine the night before. Her old jazz had soothed her mind as she'd worked out a plan. From now on, Jake Hollings would shadow her. Whatever she did, he did. Wherever she went, he went. In a way, it was punishment, but in another way, it would be therapy. The boy obviously had abandonment issues, and having her as a constant companion might help him overcome that. She planned on talking with him too, providing one-on-one therapy as they worked. Normally she had a colleague come in to talk to the boys twice a week as they worked with the horses, but Jake needed more. And if she was going to keep him safe, she was going to have to do more. As to how she was going to explain it to the other boys, she would just use his injury as an excuse.

As to how she would explain it to Grace Hollings…she wasn't quite sure on that one. On one hand, Grace would probably welcome the direct supervision, but on the other, she might become jealous. Madison had seen the color drain from her face when Jake had insisted on Madison not leaving his side. It had bit her, and hard. So no matter how she handled Jake, Grace would most likely find some reason to disapprove. But rather than this causing her anxiousness, Madison found that she almost welcomed the chance to talk to her again, and she had no idea why. The half a bottle of wine had suggested the physical attraction, and the jazz had wholeheartedly agreed. The dim light of dawn, however, had set her mind straight and such thoughts had vanished in the rising sun.

Grace Hollings was a professional, uptight, somewhat self-centered woman. She loved Jake, yes, but she wasn't truly ready to do all that was necessary to ensure his health and happiness. She was a woman focused on her job and schedule, and she was used to her life the way it was and had always been. It would take a while for her to see the light, and Madison really didn't want to be the forest she had to go through to find the trees.

She continued to watch Marv feed the colt as she lazily stroked Mazey along her tender back. "I honestly don't think he'll show. Ms. Hollings didn't seem to want him to continue on here."

"That right?"

"Yes, sir."

"Thinks it's our fault?"

"Something like that."

"According to Bobby and the other boy, he was mucking stalls and he just up and threw down his shovel, said 'I've had enough of this shit,' and took off like a bat out of hell. Bobby thought he was gonna run away. Nobody expected him to run for a horse. Especially Draco."

"Apparently, he's rather fond of Draco."

"Is he, now?"

"Yes."

Madison checked her watch as she heard a vehicle in the distance. To her surprise, it was only six thirty-five. Someone was early. She headed out for the driveway and blinked as she focused on the dust-coated black Mercedes. Grace had already climbed out wearing a navy pantsuit with a silver blouse. Her heels weren't as high, but she still had a hard time walking in them on the gravel.

"Ms. Clark." She nodded as she helped Jake emerge from the passenger side. "Good morning."

"Morning." Madison almost tipped her hat but then thought better of it. "You're early."

Grace cupped Jake's elbow as she led him closer. "Thought I'd never hear you say that."

She smiled and Madison found herself blinking again, totally moved. Grace was absolutely gorgeous. Blond and brown-eyed, creamy skin and long legs, smelling good, like heaven on a stick just standing there waiting to be consumed in every possible way.

"It's a good thing, right?" Her honey-like eyes gleamed and Madison could've sworn she was different somehow. Almost as if she'd been cleansed. And then she knew. It was evident just below the collar of her shirt. A red mark. Grace had been loved, and recently.

The realization felt like a sudden blow to her gut, and Madison struggled not to back away. She felt sick and ashamed. She shouldn't be feeling this way. She didn't even know her. What was happening? Why was everything spinning and aching?

"Come on, Jake. We have chores."

"Already?"

"Yes."

Grace seemed to fluster. “Wait. Wait, please. Will he be okay? You’ll take it easy on him, right?”

Madison couldn’t bear to look at her, the pain too great, the shame of feeling the pain overwhelming.

“Yes. He’ll be shadowing me from here on out.”

“What?” Jake’s mouth was agape.

“No arguing. You obviously need more supervision than the others, so you’re stuck with me.”

“But—”

“No arguing.”

“She’s right, Jake. And besides, you’re hurt. I’ll feel better knowing you’re with her.” She offered another smile and Madison turned away, knowing she wasn’t the true reason for it.

“You?” Jake said. “What about me? The other guys will think I’m a total baby.”

“It doesn’t matter what anyone thinks,” Madison said. “The sooner you figure that out, the better.” She clenched her jaw, so ready to move on with her day. “Let’s get going.”

“But how can I do chores with one arm?”

“I’ll show you.”

Grace tried to follow. “I’ll just leave your water out here, then?”

Jake frowned and turned to wave her off. Madison didn’t turn again at all.

“Are we mucking stalls?” Jake asked.

“Yes.”

“Really? You too?”

“Yes.”

They entered the stables and bypassed Marv and Mazey and the colt. Marv called out for her, but she ignored him and moved on. They stopped at the last stall where Draco stood and Madison had Jake watch as she put on his halter and gave him a quick rubdown. She spoke softly to him and she was glad to see that he had no reaction toward Jake. She then had Jake lead him into the empty stall across the way. Then she handed him a shovel. With Draco secure in the other stall, they started in.

"Here, shovel like this with one hand, using your body as a brace for the end of the handle."

Jake lowered his shovel and pushed as she did, using his abdomen as leverage. When he needed to lift, he used his hurt arm as a brace, leveling the grated shovel to shake and filter through the dust and hay. Madison worked next to him, pushing and shoveling as quickly as she could. When she finished, she swept and sprayed the stall down with cleaner while Jake went for the hose. She let him hose it down while she rested on a bale of hay nearby. Sweat dripped down her neck and she removed her hat to fan herself.

"What are you working so hard for?" Marv asked as the other boys milled around behind them doing their chores.

"Just doing what needs to be done."

"Thought the boy was supposed to do it."

"He is."

Marv studied Jake for a moment and then removed his own hat as well. He sat next to her.

"I think you know what's happening here, Maddy."

She grimaced. He had no clue, nor did she. Everything seemed so surreal and painful and out of control.

"It's that woman. She's getting to you."

She stood, completely offended. "You're crazy."

"No, I'm not." He shook his head and made sure no one else was within earshot. "She's driving you nuts and I can see it happening. She's got you all tangled up in this boy and their mess, and she's as stubborn as he is." He sighed. "You can't save everyone, Maddy. You just can't."

"You don't know what you're talking about."

"Every time she comes, she sets you off. You either go off and disappear or you work yourself into a tizzy. Today's another tizzy day. I can already see it."

"I'm fine."

"Only other times I've seen you like this was when—"

"Don't say it."

"I have to."

"You're wrong."

"These women do this to you, Maddy. Just as clear as day. You can't help it. And they're all the same. Hotsy-totsy, professional, own the world and everyone in it kind of women—"

"That's enough."

"I just don't want to see you go to all this trouble, getting yourself all worked up. Remember how bad it hurt the last time?"

She began to walk away, placing her hat back on her head.

"Let this go, Maddy," he continued. "You'll fall in love, and when his time's up she'll be gone."

Madison turned and marched up to him. She whispered, "I care about that boy. He's my responsibility and I, unlike everyone else in his life, will not turn my back on him just because his aunt—"

"Just because his aunt what?"

She calmed at once and backed away. "Nothing."

He stood and slapped his hat on his leg. He didn't have to say a word. He just stood there giving her the look. The one that said he saw right through her.

"I'm fine, really."

He wasn't buying it but he backed off, obviously seeing her confusion and distress. "Just feel like doing chores today?"

She nodded. He knew her so well. Too well. "Yes."

"Okay, then. I'll leave it at that."

"Thank you."

He placed a warm hand on her shoulder as he walked away. "Don't mention it."

Chapter Eleven

Can I ask you an obvious question?" May asked, slurping her Diet Coke. "Why do you care if she's rude?"

"Because I went out of my way to be nice today," Grace said, still unnerved by the morning's happenings. "I even brought Jake fifteen minutes early. I tried to joke with her. I smiled, everything. She just—God, she wouldn't even look at me."

"That is weird. Maybe she's got it bad for you."

"No, that's not it. She looked almost—disgusted, and then like maybe she was sick or something."

"Well, maybe she was."

"No, it was directed at me. For whatever reason, that woman hates me." She rubbed her forehead with the tips of her fingers. "Maybe she thinks I'm just a terrible parent to Jake. God, maybe I am. I let him stay way too long with Gabby."

"Um, excuse me, but you tried to get Jake for years because you had your suspicions. You even called protective services twice on her for surprise visits. Your mother wouldn't have it. She said everything was fine, and you know your sister put on a show every time anyone came to visit. So lay off yourself."

"I don't know." She reached down absentmindedly and scratched her collarbone.

"Oh, no."

"What?"

May pursed her lips in a playful manner as she fingered her own neck area. "You need to go check that out and cover it."

"What?"

She pointed. "That."

"What is it?"

"You tell me."

"Huh?"

"Somebody's been getting some."

Grace flushed and rose to hurry to the restroom. The pale yellow walls nearly made her panic as she stood in front of the sink and searched below her collar. And there it was. A red mark about the size of Ally Murphy's mouth. Just inside her collar.

"Oh, no." Thank God it was only May who saw it. But then another thought entered her mind, one that made her heart triple in pace. What if Madison had seen it? What if that was why she was so sickened? Of course! Now she really must think her a poor parent. Jake was hurt while she was obviously out gallivanting around. Oh God, she'd have to explain. And say what? The truth? She couldn't.

"So who is it?" May was suddenly at her side, grinning with excitement.

"No one."

"Uh-huh, right. Was she hot?"

"May, please, not now. Just help me cover it up."

"Way ahead of you, woman." May slipped out a compact, opened Grace's shirt, and began patting on powder foundation.

"Is it really noticeable?" Had everyone seen it? Even when she'd walked in and said good morning? Ugh. How unprofessional. How irresponsible. How—she couldn't even think about it. She just wanted it gone.

"You couldn't see all of it, but you could see enough. Any moron would've known what it was."

Grace hesitated and then voiced her fear, needing confirmation that she was indeed just paranoid and insane, instead of oh fuck, unimaginably right. "I think maybe Madison Clark may have seen it."

"What?"

Yes, the idea was indeed ridiculous. Oh, thank the heavens, she agreed.

But May's face twisted in both horror and excitement. "Oh my God, you're right! She—" She poked her finger at Grace's chest. "She saw it and she got jealous."

"What? No." What the hell?

"Yes, it makes perfect sense." She hopped up and down slightly with her newfound theme. "She saw the hickey and it pissed her off because it made her jealous to think of you with another. She wants you, woman. I knew it. All the rudeness and ignoring. It's classic outward denial caused by classic inner interest. It's so junior high 101."

Grace was about to argue, but her mind clouded with May's words. Jealous? Madison? Really? Could her look have been one of stung jealousy? Was it possible? The mere possibility made her stomach flip-flop with nerves.

"No, she's not like that. Trust me."

"You're unsure, though, aren't you? I can see it in your eyes. There is a possibility."

She shook her head. "If you could see her, the way she acts around me—I just don't think it's jealousy or anything like that." But then there was that moment in the hospital. The briefest of moments where they'd stared into each other and their breathing had quickened.

"What if it is?" May asked.

What if it was? What would she do? How would she find out? She wouldn't, because the plain and simple fact was that Madison was disgusted by her, hickey or no hickey. There was nothing further. She'd made it more than obvious that morning.

"Madison Clark does not like me," she said for May's benefit as well as her own. "And that's the reality of it."

"How do you explain her actions toward you?" May patted Grace's skin with her fingertips, then backed away to give her approval.

"She doesn't like me. End of story."

"I meant today's actions. She saw that mark, Grace. She had to have."

"Even if she did, it only disgusted her. She probably assumed I was out getting a piece of ass while Jake was home hurt."

"Did you?"

"Please."

"I'm just asking."

"No."

"Okay. So the ass came to you."

"May, please."

"Why don't you tell me anything anymore? My life is so boring without your stories."

"Fine, the ass—the woman came to me. Okay? It wasn't planned and I probably shouldn't have let it happen. But it did."

"Was it hot?"

"It was—sex."

"Oh, yeah. Hot."

"May."

"Sorry. So what does this mean?"

"What does what mean?"

"The sex? Is it someone I know? Is it going to continue as a casual thing?"

"No, it was a mistake. I mean, it was good and all, but I have Jake to think about, and this case."

"True." May helped her close her shirt. "Still, it was good. Who is she?"

"An acquaintance."

"Well, obviously."

"You don't know her." It was true, May was not friends with Ally, nor had they ever worked together on a case. But still she wasn't about to tell. May was many things, and a gossip wasn't usually one of them. But Grace didn't want to take any chances, nor did she want to have to explain.

"Just someone I dated once or twice who happened to stop by for a nightcap to catch up."

"I see."

"What about you?" Grace checked her reflection and was pleased to find that the mark had been expertly covered. Now she could relax. She could shrug back into her suit jacket and go get Jake without a care in the world when the time came. "Still no dates?"

They left the restroom to return to Grace's office. "No."

"Why not?"

"Just no one I'm into. They're all metrosexual babies more concerned with their appearance than mine."

"You're dating the wrong ones."

"You always say that."

"And you always say that to me."

Her eyes flickered with wicked intent. "Then let's change it up. I pick your dates and you pick mine."

Grace rolled her eyes. "What on earth makes you think I'd agree to that?"

"Because it will be fun, and for once you get to approve of my date and vice versa."

"I told you, I don't have time to date."

"Come on, just once. Humor me? I already have someone in mind."

"You couldn't possibly."

"I do."

"Who?" Grace sat and crossed her legs. She foresaw her temples throbbing, so she immediately delved into Janine's famous, wonderful, heavenly, life-saving coffee.

"Joe said his friend Juan was looking for a lesbian to go on a date with his friend."

"Are you kidding me? I didn't even understand that. And the answer is no."

"You didn't let me finish. I guess she's really cool, has her own business, she's a psychologist, somewhat wealthy, very attractive, and drives a BMW."

"So?"

"So? She sounds perfect."

"You don't even know the woman or Juan, for God's sake."

"I know Juan. He's super nice. I guess he's going to be dating this woman's best friend and they need a date for her."

"Great, she can't get a date? A blind one at that? And you want me to go? Come on, May."

May laughed. "I know it sounds ridiculous, but she really does sound nice. From what I hear she doesn't want to go either, but her friend is making her."

"Sounds familiar."

"What do you have to lose?"

"Pride, self-respect, a whole evening."

"I'll find out more."

"Don't bother, I'm not going."

"What if I get a pic?" May asked, playful eyebrow raised.

"Wouldn't matter."

"Uh-huh, we'll see."

"Yeah, we'll see all right." She powered up her laptop. "Switch gears. We gotta get to work."

❖

Evening had yet to settle in when Grace pulled up at the ranch at five till four. The air was oven warm and the breeze too teasing to be considered polite. But the sky was bright blue with a spattering of fluffy clouds, and the horses looked beautiful against the purple mountain backdrop. Despite knowing she had to face Madison, Grace found herself breathing deep and allowing the day's stresses to slip away. Maybe this place wasn't so bad after all.

She slid her hands into her pockets and looked around. Several boys stood with Madison near the stable, so she steered clear and focused on a nearby pen where the cowboy she'd seen before was working with a baby horse.

She approached and smiled. "Is that the same horse Jake helped you bottle-feed before?"

The cowboy looked up but seemed unimpressed. "Same one." Grace wondered if being rude was in the water around there.

"What's his name?"

"Ain't got one."

"Why not?"

The cowboy removed his hat to scratch his head. "Hasn't told us yet."

"Who hasn't, Madison? I mean Ms. Clark?"

He chuckled. "Nah. The horse." He continued to stroke his ribs.

"Oh, I see." She rounded the pen to the entrance where she opened the gate. "Is it a boy or girl? A colt's a boy, right?"

"Yes, ma'am."

At least I got that right. "Can I pet him?"

He patted the baby's neck and stood. "I don't know."

"Well, why not?"

"He's not exactly hand tamed yet. Might nip ya."

She guffawed. "I think I can handle petting a baby horse."

The cowboy backed off. "Suit yourself. But don't say I didn't warn you."

"I don't need warning." She walked up to the horse and knelt by his side. The sun was heating his pelt and she could smell the earthy scent of him. When she touched him he felt as warm as he smelled. "Hi," she said sweetly. He shifted a little and one ear went back. "It's okay. I just want to pet you." She reached out and stroked his neck, amazed at the soft yet firm feel of him. One eye stared at her and it was so black and liquid she could see herself in it. "You're beautiful," she whispered. And in that moment she felt him within her chest and her heart sped up. She could feel his heart kick as well as she touched his ribs.

"He's scared," she said to no one in particular. "But not of me," she said softly to herself. She kept stroking him and staring into his eye. She could sense him somehow, his trepidation, his worry, his longing. Her chest warmed and then she felt a drop within and she knew the feeling all too well. It was the same feeling she got when she thought about Jake.

"What's going on here?"

Grace jumped up and the horse kicked and took off, clocking

her in her knee. At once she hopped on one foot, lost her balance on her high heel, and fell on her ass in the dirt. "Ouch, God dang it." She held her knee to her chest and cursed. The cowboy was immediately at her side, cupping her elbow.

"Come on now." He eased her up and over to the side of the pen. Grace limped slightly, the pain of stretching her leg making itself known. She saw Madison with an angry look on her face as she hurried after the horse. When she caught him by the rope, she handed him off to another young man.

"Put him in with Mazey."

"Yes, ma'am." He walked quickly with the horse and left the pen. Madison, however, was staring her down, as was Jake, who was leaning on the bars of the pen.

Grace quickly brushed off her backside and her clothing, tucking loose strands of hair behind her ears. She knew she must look a wreck.

"What the hell just happened?" Madison asked, looking directly at her.

"I was petting the baby horse."

"I can see that," Madison said, mouth slightly open as she nodded in anger. "But why?"

"Why?" Was she stupid? "He's cute and I love ani—"

"I told her she could," Marv mumbled. "Damn stupid of me, obviously."

"Wait, no." Grace held up a palm. "Everything was fine until you walked up and shouted." She aimed the comment at Madison.

"I didn't shout."

"Yes, you did." It had nearly scared her to death.

"No, she didn't," Jake voiced.

She turned on him and gave him a *give me a break* look.

Hadn't she yelled?

"Look, whatever. I just know I was fine until you came along and said what you said."

"So it's my fault you scared my foal half to death?"

"I—whatever." She hated the look on her face, and when she saw Madison's eyes drift down to her collar and back up again quickly, she knew exactly why. Madison Clark didn't like her. In any way whatsoever. And she'd probably felt that way from the beginning, but when she saw the mark earlier that morning, she'd solidified it. "The mark is gone, so don't bother looking."

Madison blinked at her, showing she'd understood the words but refused to give meaning to them. "I think you'd better go."

"I think so too."

But damn it if she didn't look so good mad. Grace wanted to tear her own hair out for thinking so, especially since her insides were on fire with anger. But Madison Clark was Madison Clark, and anger touched her skin like desire, brushing her cheeks and neck with deep red. Her eyes burned hotter than the sun, causing her irises to nearly sizzle and mist outward like water evaporating.

Grace stared her down, partly out of pride and anger and partly out of a need to watch her.

"I did good today, Aunt Grace."

Jake was speaking, but he sounded far away.

"Admit it," Grace said to her, needing to know. "Admit you were looking for the mark." *Admit that's part of the reason why you hate me, despise me, are so rude to me. Admit that you judge me.*

"I don't know what you're talking about." Her eyes cooled at once and turned to dark stone.

"The mark, the one near my collar. The one you saw this morning and were looking for again."

Madison clenched her jaw and walked away. She said, "Jake's talking to you," as she passed by.

"Thank you, I heard him." But when she looked to him, he was staring at her in even more anger than before. He looked so red and puffed up she thought his head might explode. "Let's go," she said.

"No."

She moved out of the gate. "Jake, let's go. I'm not playing around."

"I don't want to go with you."

"Jake," she sighed. "I'm sorry you had to see that. I'm just upset."

"Why are you talking about marks?" His face contorted. "What does that even mean? You embarrass me," he said as he took off toward the car.

"Jake," she called after him, but it was no use. He climbed in the car and slammed the door. She leaned on the bars to catch her breath and saw the cowboy watching her. "Thanks for letting me pet the horse. He's sweet."

He twirled his long mustache between his fingers. "Yeah. He's something all right." He stared at her with piercing blue eyes behind wedges of tan skin. Then he pushed off from the bars. "That mark you're talking about?"

"Yeah?" she called after him.

"It red?"

"Yes. Why?"

"It's right there on your chest just as plain as day."

CHAPTER TWELVE

Morning, Jake," Madison said as he walked slowly toward her and the other boys. He still wore his splint, but he was dressed appropriately in jeans, work boots, hat, and T-shirt. The sun had darkened his fair skin to a reddish brown.

"Morning, ma'am." He placed his water container at his feet and Madison stared out at the black Mercedes where Grace remained. After a few seconds, she turned the car around and left, not bothering to get out. Most guardians did the same thing after a few days, but Madison wondered if Grace was staying away because of their encounter the evening before. She'd gone over it in her mind all night long. How had Grace known she'd seen the mark? Had she seen her looking? Had she seen her look that morning? Had she wanted her to see it? The questions remained, and none of the answers made sense. Unless Grace somehow thought Madison was interested in her. Otherwise why would she care? None of it made sense. Madison had never shown any interest in her. She wouldn't dare. So was Grace convinced Madison was gay and had a thing for her?

It angered her to think so. It was quite an assumption, and what gave her the right to assume such a thing? The EMT? Just because she was gay didn't mean she had an interest in every woman that came along.

"Ma'am?" one of the boys asked, bringing her back around.

"Yes?"

"Should we go clock in, or is there something we should know?"

How long was I spacing out? "Go ahead and clock in. Start in on your chores. Michael, your chores have changed a bit. Jake, you're still with me."

The boys dispersed and Madison headed toward the hay truck with Jake on her heels. Every morning Bobby and some of the other boys filled the truck and backed it up toward the pens. And every morning Madison and the boys dispersed it.

"I'll help you," she said to Jake as she grabbed one end of a thirty-pound bale of Bermuda hay. Jake helped as best he could, shoving both arms under and lifting. She could see the strain on his face. "Good, now hang on. We're going right into the first pen. Good job. Hang on. Now bend your knees and place it in the container." They knelt and dropped it in. Then she fished out her box cutter and sliced the strings. "Now let's spread these flakes around to the other containers."

She had four large rubber containers in this pen, three in another, and two in the last pen. The first was for the horses who got along well but needed to be separated from the horses in pen two. Horses were like people, and sometimes they preferred their friends over others. She tried her best to keep the harmony. Pen three was for Draco and any other horse who needed to be alone until he was better socialized. That wasn't the case now, though, and she saw Jake staring off at the black gelding as he trotted around his pen.

"Ready for another one?" She helped him disperse the hay throughout the containers.

"You mean another ride on Draco?"

"Noooo."

He turned to look at her and his smile fell. "Oh, you mean hay. Sure." They moved back toward the truck.

"You really like Draco, don't you?" she asked.

"I guess."

"I think you do, and that's okay."

"It is?"

"Sure. He's a beautiful boy."

He looked off toward him again. "Yeah, but it's more than that."

She shifted a bale. "How do you mean?"

"I don't know. I just really like him."

She watched as he stared at the horse for a few more seconds. "Come on now, here we go." But as she motioned for him to help, he surprised her by lifting one on his own. "You sure you got it?"

"Yeah," he grunted. She grabbed another bale and led the way to the other pens. When they placed the bales in the containers, she handed over her blade.

"Go ahead. Cut the strings."

He took the knife and eased up the blade. She held the string taut and instructed him to cut. When he did, he grinned.

"Now let's do the other one."

He concentrated intently as he cut the other string.

"Good job," she said, always giving encouragement. The boys needed that more than almost anything, and this one was starving for it.

"Can we do some more?" He returned the cutter to her and his eyes danced. "After we spread this around?"

"Not this morning."

His eyes lowered in disappointment.

"We're going to be working with Draco."

"Really?" His gaze came back up and his shoulders straightened.

"Yep."

"What are we going to do?"

They spread the hay around to various containers as other boys came out with water hoses to clean and fill the troughs.

"First we're going to rub him down and see how he reacts. Then I'll try a harness again."

"What for?"

"Well, we're trying to get him saddle broke."

"Oh."

"And after your little escapade, he's fighting the bit and rein."

Jake grew quiet. "You think I scared him?"

"Wouldn't that have scared you?"

"Yeah, I guess so."

They entered Draco's pen and the horse lifted his front hoof and brushed the ground with it several times. His ears went back and Madison encouraged Jake to wait by the gate. She moved toward him cautiously, hands out by her side. She called softly and when his ears flickered forward, she smiled. "That's a boy, Draco." She stroked his velvety muzzle and moved down to his strong neck. He smelled of hay and dust and his nose was slightly wet as she kissed it.

"Come on over, Jake," she said, careful not to be too loud. He moved carefully and he had a look of profound sadness on his face. "What's wrong?" she asked.

"I made him scared." He stood in front of the horse, looking intently into his face. "I'm sorry, boy."

Madison didn't say anything, knowing this was a pivotal moment. Jake was feeling empathy for the horse. This was huge. "Here." She took his good hand and placed it on Draco's neck. "Pet him softly. Tell him why you did it."

"Why?" He looked at her curiously, without sarcasm.

"Because he'll listen."

"But he can't understand."

"He understands more than you think."

"But how?"

She moved back to stroke Draco's ribs and flank, running her fingers through his mane from time to time. "Horses can sense things about people. Just like how you can sense things about him."

"I never thought of it that way."

"You're drawn to Draco, aren't you? You like him a lot?"

"Yeah." The sun glinted off the blond hair sticking out around his hat. She avoided his eyes, knowing they looked too much like his aunt's.

"Well, I think Draco likes you too."

"No way."

"Yes, I think he does. The other boys make him nervous. But

you—he's different around you. Even after your escapade." She smiled. "He's letting you pet him, isn't he?"

"He doesn't with the others?"

"No. He lets them walk him and lead him around. But petting for Draco is special. And he's very antsy about who he lets near him."

"How come?"

She encouraged him to rub him firmer to help stimulate his circulation. Draco snorted and shifted his pelt in approval.

"I'm glad you asked. You see, Jake, Draco hasn't had an easy life. He's been beaten and starved and neglected. No one has ever really cared for him or about him until now."

"Is that why he's so—unfriendly?"

"I would imagine so. Wouldn't it make you unfriendly and unable to trust people?"

He thought for a long moment. "Yeah. It does make me like that. You just think no one gives a crap even when they do. It's just easier to push them away."

"That way you don't take the risk and you don't get hurt."

He nodded. "Yeah."

"Well, what do you think about Draco? Should he take the risk with you?"

He started to nod but then stopped. "I don't know. I already did something bad by taking him."

"Well, tell him why you took him. He might understand."

"I—I just wanted to take off. And I wanted him to be the one to go with me."

"Why did you want to take off?"

"Because I was mad about the chores and about having to be here. I just wanted to run."

"Where were you going?" She retrieved two brushes from a nearby bin and handed him one to use on Draco.

"I don't know. Just away."

"The desert?"

He shrugged. "I guess. I really didn't think that far."

"Just a spur of the moment, so to speak?"

"Yeah."

"One of the things about growing up, Jake, is that you have to think ahead. Every action you take will lead to something. Here, take the currycomb. Use this first to loosen any dirt or sweat." She showed him how to brush vigorously.

"What if you just don't care?"

"You have to care. Or you'll end up in serious trouble." She studied him carefully, making sure he was listening. "I'm not just talking about jail or juvie. I'm talking about serious, life-threatening trouble."

He looked at her with questions in his eyes. She explained.

"If Draco had bucked you harder or you had fallen differently, you could've broken bones, broken your neck, even been paralyzed. Can you imagine not being able to walk?"

"No, I don't want to."

"What if you had managed to get to the desert? You would've been without shade or water for miles. You would've been dehydrated—"

"At the time I didn't care what happened to me."

"Well, what about Draco? You wouldn't have wanted that to happen to him, would you?"

"No."

"There you go. You've got to think. Not just about you but about how what you do affects everyone and everything around you."

He kept brushing and she could tell he was thinking. She hoped she was reaching him.

"I would've cared if something had happened to you, Jake. And so would your aunt and everyone here."

"Really?"

"Yes."

"Why?" His question was serious. He really had no idea why she or anyone else would care.

"Because I like you. I care about you. I don't want to see bad things happen to you."

"You don't?"

"No. Just like how you wouldn't want to see bad things happen to anyone you care about. Like your mom or aunt."

He scoffed. "My mom, I've seen so many bad things happen to her already."

"It made you feel bad, didn't it? Worried. Scared."

"Yeah. But after a while it stopped mattering."

"You shut off inside."

He shrugged.

"What about your aunt? You care about her?"

She hesitated in bringing up Grace, but she told herself it was to help Jake.

"Yeah, she's all right, I guess."

"Just all right? She's good to you, isn't she?"

"I guess. I mean she's good about getting me stuff and everything, but she works a lot."

"Most people have to."

"No, I mean a lot. She's always at work and when she's not, she's at home on her laptop working, always talking to herself."

Madison laughed a little at that. "Talking to herself?"

He laughed too. "Yeah, especially when she's working. Which is, like, all the time."

"Maybe you should tell her you'd like to spend more time with her."

"And do what?"

"I don't know. What would you like to do with her?" She brushed Draco quick and short with the stiff brush alongside Jake. "This brush gets rid of all the stuff you just loosened," she said.

"Okay, makes sense."

"What would you like to do with her?"

"Beats me," he said.

"You like movies?"

"Yeah."

"Ask her to a movie." She tried not to think of taking Grace to a movie. The big dark room, the inability for Grace to say anything offensive, the way she would look in the screen light, her elegant hand just sitting there waiting for Madison to take it.

"Or whatever you think is fun."

"Video games?" His face lit up.

"Er, I don't know. Would your aunt like that?"

He laughed. "No. Would you?"

"This isn't about me."

"Come on, would you? What if it was at one of those big game places where they have games and go-karts and all that?"

She nodded. "Yeah, that sounds like fun."

"Cool."

"Your aunt would probably like that too."

"Think so?"

"Sure. You should ask her. Go have some fun."

"I might do that." He spat and squinted into the sun. "Did Draco really get beat?"

They walked the length of pen, stroking Draco as they moved.

"Yes, Jake, I'm afraid so."

"Why would anyone beat a horse?"

"Why would anyone beat anything?"

"'Cuz they're mad?"

"Anger can be controlled and expressed in other ways."

"Like how?"

"Like running."

He smiled and she returned it. "Or doing any kind of hard, physical work, for that matter."

"Like rugby," Rob said loudly as he approached from near the drive.

She grinned and agreed. "Or like rugby."

"What's rugby?" Jake asked.

"What's rugby?" Rob clenched his chest as if in heart pain. "These new boys are killing me, Madness."

"Madness?" Jake suddenly had a grin of his own.

"It's her nickname. 'Cause she's so temperamental," Rob said.

"Don't tell him that. He'll believe it."

"Well, you are. You're a regular old hothead. Always screaming and throwing stuff about."

She laughed. "Okay, sure, that's me."

"Are you kidding? She's, like, the calmest person I know," Jake said.

"Ooh, the young knight comes to your defense. Impressive."

"He's kidding, Jake."

"I hope so. After all that talk about anger."

"You were going to make me run laps?" she said, slapping Jake lightly on the back.

"Yeah!" He liked the idea of that.

"So who is this young valiant? Judging by the splint I'd say this has to be Jake."

"Jake Hollings, meet Rob Sheffield. Rob's our vet and he just happens to be Mr. Rugby extraordinaire."

"Rugby's like football," Rob said, leaning on the bars of the pen. "Only it's for real warriors. No pads."

"Wow." Jake stared at him for a moment and Madison took Draco. She slipped off his harness after leading him to his hay. She continued to rub him down.

"Another one interested!" Rob said, smiling. "You can't keep them from me, Madness, you just can't."

"Apparently not."

"You, young man," Rob shook his hand as Jake neared the bars, "can come to a practice whenever you want and check it out."

"There's really no pads?"

"No pads. Just meat and bones, buddy. And sweat and grit."

"I could tackle other guys and stuff?"

"Yes, and they can tackle you. You can get hit pretty hard. You sure you're up for something like that?"

Jake puffed out his chest. "Yes."

"Okay, then. We'll see you at practice sometime so you can see for yourself."

"Sure."

Madison piped in. "He'll have to ask his aunt."

Jake didn't seem to like the sound of that. "She'll say yes. She better."

"Remember what I said, Jake," Madison said. "About thinking about others."

He looked down, spat, and covered the mark with dirt. "Yeah, okay. I'll ask her if she'll go with me."

"You two could watch the practice together. We always scrimmage," Rob said.

"I'll be sure to give his aunt the info," Madison said. "Jake, go find Bobby and see if any stalls still need cleaning. I'll be along shortly to give you a hand."

"Yes, ma'am." He walked away slowly, giving Draco a last longing look.

"He doesn't seem so tough," Rob said when he was out of earshot.

"I don't think he is. I just think he *thinks* he is."

"I see. Showing some forced machismo, huh?"

"Yes."

"Trying to hide all that anger and insecurity."

"Afraid so."

"He seems to be doing well, though. He listened to you. And I can't believe how calm Draco is with him."

"You noticed that, did you? Well, you know what they say. Horses can sense those like them."

"Boy, if that isn't true."

"Know what I think? I think he's got something special." She exited the pen and they headed for the shade of the patio. As Rob sat she poured them both some watered-down iced tea. It tasted crisp and cool with just a hint of the mint she'd placed on the top of their full glasses.

"Think so?"

"Mmm-hmm. I've been thinking about it for a while. The way he is with Draco…he shows a lot of sensitivity. And there's something else too. He has a strange calm about him when he's with the horses. It makes them feel at ease."

"Like Marv?"

"Sort of. But with less hands on."

"That's great. Has he said anything about it yet?"

"I told him I thought Draco was great around him. That Draco isn't so at ease with the other boys."

"What did he say?"

"Not much."

"Maybe he doesn't understand how cool that is."

"Probably not."

Once again, Grace came to her mind. "Thing is, yesterday, I saw his aunt with the colt and it was the same kind of thing. He was so at ease with her. Until…"

His eyebrow arched and he sat forward with elbows on the table.

"Well, until I came up on them and scared her."

"What happened?"

"She jumped, the colt kicked her in the knee, and she fell on her butt."

He covered his mouth and tried not to laugh. "Madness, that's terrible."

"I didn't mean to. I saw her with that colt and remembered the way she'd yelled at us over Jake, and I lost it. I wondered what the hell *she* was doing unsupervised with a horse."

"She was in there alone?"

"Marv was watching."

"So she wasn't alone."

"Have you seen that colt? He's feisty."

"Madness, you scared the shit out of her." He laughed fully. "For no good reason!"

"She shouldn't be in there with him! She's an attorney, for Christ's sake."

"So?"

"So I'm afraid she'll get sue happy. She already hates me."

"What makes you think that she's that kind of person?"

"Because of how she was when Jake took off on Draco. Her first reaction was to blame us."

"She's a mother, Madness. Or like his mother."

"Okay, I'll give you that one, but she's so rude to me. Yesterday she—"

"Got kicked after you scared the shit out of her and the colt?"

"Yes. But she also…"

His eyebrow arched again. "Yes?"

"She started in on me about this mark she had on her chest."

"What! Oh, this is something I have to hear!"

"Okay, she had this mark just inside her collar. It looked like a hickey and she caught me looking at it."

"Okaaay."

"She said the mark is gone so you don't need to look for it."

"Huh?"

"She thought I, she thought I saw it that morning."

"Did you?"

"Yes." Her voice had given her away.

"And you looked at it."

"Well, yes."

"And you looked at it again last evening?"

"It was as plain as day."

"Madness." He folded his hands and rested his chin on them. "Is this woman attractive?"

"What does that have to do with anything?"

"I knew it! I so knew it." He glanced around to make sure they were alone. "Is she gay?"

"I seriously doubt it."

"But she obviously knows you are."

"Am I that obvious?"

"In that attire and with your build? Yes, honey. And she knows. Otherwise, why care if you see her hickey? She must think you're interested. Or be afraid you're interested."

"Great, wonderful."

"Or she's embarrassed by it. Or…" He wagged a finger at her. "She was ashamed of what you thought. Or—"

"How many of these ors are there?"

"One more. She likes you."

Madison's heart careened in excitement and then fell in disappointment. "No way."

He studied her for a long moment as if trying to decipher her thoughts. "Could be. Being embarrassed about it is one thing. But confronting you on it is another. Tell me, what did you do when you first saw it?"

"I don't know. I think I looked away."

"Did you blush?"

"No—well, I felt my face heat."

That brought a knowing smile to his face, so she quickly explained, "But not from embarrassment."

The smile remained. "Then from what?"

"I was—upset."

"Aha! Madness, you like her!"

"No, I don't. I don't. I promise you I don't." But who was she trying to convince, herself or Rob?

"Then what?"

"I think I got upset because she was obviously messing around while Jake was hurt."

"That is the most ridiculous thing I've ever heard."

"Why?"

"Because you don't know her living situation. She may have a lover, a boyfriend, a girlfriend. And none of those suggest she isn't taking care of her kid. I think you just got jealous."

"I'm not jealous."

"Are too. You like her."

"Rob, I swear to God." Her resolve was failing, and she knew he could sense it.

"Okay, so prove it."

She stuck out her chin, determined to make the stirring and maddening feelings stop. "How?"

"Go on that date with me." He wiggled his eyebrows. "I found someone."

"Oh, please, not this again."

"You promised."

"Well, now that you actually expect it to happen, I'm backing out."

"No, you're not. This one's a real winner. And supposedly quite the stunner. Wanna know more?" His championship rugby ring glinted in the sunlight, along with his dancing eyes.

"No." The last thing she needed was another woman thrown into the mix.

"Okay, your choice. But we're going. Saturday night at six."

She groaned and downed the rest of her iced tea. The day was growing hotter by the second and she needed to get back to Jake. They had fencing to repair, weeds to pull, and more supplies to order.

"If anything, it will be good to get out. You know, go have a nice dinner."

"Sometimes I really hate you."

"I know. But only when I make you do things you're afraid of."

She stared at him in disbelief. "Oh, really? Is that what you think?"

"I just call 'em as I see 'em, Madness."

"Well, fine. I'll go on that damn date. But this means you'll back off for a while with the whole 'Madison is so alone' crap." It also included talk of Grace, but she was too afraid to bring her up again for fear he'd see right through her.

"Okay."

"I'm talking months. Six at least."

"Deal."

"Good." She stood and stretched, placing her hat on her head.

"Let's go look at that little boy," Rob said, standing alongside her, referring to the colt. "How's he been doing?"

Madison walked quickly as her mind stumbled over Grace, the blind date, and Jake all at once. At least after Saturday she could put one to rest.

"He's doing better than me."

Rob laughed.

Madison wasn't kidding.

Chapter Thirteen

I don't think I should go," Grace said as she hurriedly let May inside the front door.

"Why not?" May scooted in wearing neatly pressed shorts and a soft blouse. Painted toenails showed through her cute leather sandals.

Grace led her in further where she gestured toward the sofa. May set down her purse but stood with her hands on her hips. "There's no way you're not going. You need this, Grace. You need to do something for yourself."

"But Jake is here. And he's hurt."

"He's fine. You said yourself he's been working hard at the ranch, even with one arm. If he can do that, he can sure as hell sit around with me like a bump on a log." She held up her large purse. "I even brought scary movies. Five of them. And…" She dug through her bag. "Microwave popcorn. And…" She dug some more. "Milk Duds. What kid doesn't like Milk Duds?"

"Kids with braces."

"Oh, shit. He doesn't have braces, right? I don't remember him having braces."

"He doesn't."

She sighed. "Good. So you're going."

"I don't know anyone, May. Do you know how stressful that is?"

"You spoke to Juan on the phone. He's nice. He'll look out for you."

"I'm going to dinner with three complete strangers." The mere idea nearly cramped her stomach.

She didn't seem to have an answer for that one, and Grace was beginning to sweat despite her short, tight dress.

"You'll be fine. Just pretend like it's the courtroom and they're the jury. Win them over. You're great at that. And you look gorgeous. Where did you get that dress?"

"Nieman Marcus."

"And the shoes are drop-dead. God, even I want you right now."

The dress was a simple sheath with three cutouts in the neckline. Short, black, and extremely fitted. Her heels matched: strappy, high, and black. Shimmering lotion covered her body along with her favorite perfume, Gio. She wore her hair down, and its thick, flowing waves contrasted nicely with the black of her dress. Her smoky eye shadow brought out her eyes and her lipstick was a deep red. For someone who didn't even really want to go, she was sure going all out.

"It will probably be a disappointment," she said, knowing she'd probably got all dressed up for nothing.

"Most blind dates are. But there is always that one shot. That lightning-strike chance you will find the love of your life."

"Right. I'd have a better chance of lightning itself actually hitting me. Do I really have to go?"

"Yes."

She sighed.

"You'll be fine. You might even have fun."

"Ha."

She checked the mirror in the entryway, rubbed her teeth free of lipstick, and took a deep breath. "Okay, I'm going."

"We won't wait up," May said in a high-pitched playful voice.

"I won't be gone long," she replied back in a similar tone. "Bye, Jake!" she yelled toward the hallway.

"Later!" came the distant reply.

He was playing video games again, all sprawled out on his bed. When she'd told him about going on a blind date, he'd merely laughed and said good luck. And when she'd reminded him it was with a woman, he'd scoffed and wished her even more luck.

"He's playing games," she said to May. "So you'll be lucky if you even see those movies."

"I have my ways." She came to the door and placed her hand on Grace's bare shoulder. "Now run along. I have your number, I won't have any boys over, and I won't tie up the phone line."

"Good." She managed to laugh a little. God, she was nervous. "Bye."

"Bye!" May shooed her out the door and nearly slammed it in her face.

"Guess she really does want me to go on this date." Grace climbed in her Mercedes and drove as slowly as she could to the restaurant. It wasn't too far and traffic wasn't bad, but she wanted to put off arriving as long as she could. If she showed up early, she'd look desperate and she would feel exposed standing there alone. If she arrived late, she'd feel embarrassed as everyone watched and waited for her to approach. So the key was to arrive right on time, precisely with the others. A quick glance at her clock told her she was timing her arrival perfectly, but it didn't help to settle her nerves any. They doubled in ferocity as she pulled into the restaurant and found the lot jammed full of cars. Saturday nights in Phoenix were crazy at popular restaurants, and she both hoped and didn't hope that Juan had made reservations. If he made them and the woman was nice, then they'd hopefully be seated right away. If he didn't, well, then she could go home and forget this whole thing, regardless how the woman was. After her brief encounter with Ally she didn't feel the need to have anyone in her life right now. She was too busy, not to mention Jake.

"So why am I here?" she groaned after swinging into a rare parking space. "Because I'm a fool and I listen to May, that's why." She checked her reflection in her vanity mirror. Luckily, her face didn't show her nerves. It never did and it had earned her the nickname the "woman of steel" by a few people she worked with, mainly opposing attorneys.

"Woman of steel, here you go," she said as she climbed from

the vehicle. With a deep breath and a straightening of her spine, she headed for the entrance. The sun had yet to settle, so she kept on her designer sunglasses as she approached. She felt somewhat safe behind them and hoped she could meet her companions with them still on. Woman of steel or not, it would be nice to hide her eyes for a while. But unfortunately and as she'd suspected, they weren't waiting outside. Slipping off her shades, she walked in as a man held the door for her. He looked at her hungrily, but she was used to that and looked away after a polite thank you. The lobby was full of people and she began scanning faces. More looks came her way, mostly from men. But which one was Juan?

"Grace?" She turned and found a small Hispanic-looking man smiling at her. He looked friendly and pleasant and he took her hand in his. "Joe said to look for the blond bombshell dressed to the nines."

"Hi." She shook his warm hand.

"Guess he was right, wow. You look wonderful." He brought her in for a kiss on the cheek.

"Thank you," she said.

He looked nice himself in a pressed oxford-style Ralph Lauren shirt and khaki pants. His loafers gleamed and he smelled nice too. Like papaya lotion of some sort. "You look dashing yourself."

"Why, thank you." He turned slightly and reached for another man, this one taller and thicker with muscle. "Grace, this is Rob. Rob, Grace."

"Hello, Grace." He had a gorgeous smile with a dimple on one side, and his hand was massive as it gently took hers.

"Rob, it's a pleasure." Her pulse raced as she searched for her date.

Rob caught her glance. "She's not here quite yet."

"Oh."

"In fact…" He looked at his watch and his muscles bulged under his tight-fitting short-sleeved collared shirt. "If I didn't know any better, I'd say she's probably sitting in her car and debating whether or not to come in."

"Sounds familiar," she said.

"Aw, don't be nervous," Juan said, taking her arm. "Rob said she's one of the most caring people you'll ever meet. Besides, you have me, and I know I'm nice."

She laughed. "Yes, I think you are. Thank you."

He winked.

"Here she is," Rob said and she and Juan turned to look. Grace's heart fluttered a little as she watched a strong-looking woman with short dirty blond hair embrace him. When they released and the woman turned to look at her, Grace nearly fell.

"Madison, this is Grace," Rob said.

Madison too appeared to stop in her tracks and stare. The color drained from her face, showing she was just as shocked to see Grace as Grace was to see her.

Grace kept blinking, making sure it was her. Madison looked so different in a stylish stand-alone white blazer with thick brown buttons and matching bead necklace. Her jeans were dark with a modern cut, low rise on the hips where a hint of a brown belt showed. Her shoes were brown, square toed with a thick heel. So well put together and so casually elegant. She was…absolutely gorgeous.

"Madison," Grace whispered. Wait. Her date was Madison? Madison Clark? What the hell—

"Nice to see you, Grace," Madison said, shocking her again by coming to take her hand. "You look…" Her eyes twinkled with intensity. "Very nice."

"You two know each other?" Now it was Rob's turn to be shocked.

"No—yes." They seemed to answer in unison.

"We don't really know each other," Grace explained.

Rob and Juan appeared lost.

"I know Grace through the ranch," Madison said, clearing a tight-sounding throat.

Grace quickly explained. "My nephew Jake, uh, goes to the ranch."

"Oh," Rob said in a high voice, trying too hard to act surprised at the news. Had he heard of her? He shot Madison a quick look as the maître d' called his name and they headed for their table.

He has heard of me. Oh God.

She wanted to run. Madison must too. She should say something. Without trying to garner too much attention, she fell back and slightly touched Madison's arm.

"Should I go?" she whispered.

"Go where?"

"Home."

Madison just stared at her with eyes that were set off by her thick hair. Grace suddenly hated the cowboy hat and bandana. They did her no justice whatsoever.

"Am I that bad?" Madison asked.

"Excuse me?"

"Never mind. You can go if you want."

"No, I think you misunderstood. I—"

But the men were waiting for them, standing patiently by their chairs.

"I thought you might want me to go," Grace added quickly. Madison was looking beyond her at their table.

"Don't be ridiculous," she said in a tone that Grace couldn't read. "We can have dinner. We aren't barbarians. Are we?" The look she gave her suggested Grace might think she was or vice versa. It was difficult to tell. Whatever it was, it was definitely a knowing look, one full of hidden or secret knowledge. Grace wished she'd let her in on it.

"Of course not." *Am I?* She thought back to her two falls, the hickey, and the way they'd spoken to each other. *Maybe I have behaved badly.*

"Then by all means," Madison said, encouraging her to go first.

They joined Juan and Rob at the table and sat quietly. Rob kept smiling at her while Juan did his best at conversation. Grace tried not to act nervous, but sitting next to Madison had her insides stirring like a ball of hot chaos. She didn't know if it was the way she looked or simply the fact that it was Madison Clark. Whatever the reason, she was a wad of misfiring nerves.

"So, Grace, what kind of law do you practice?" Rob finally asked.

"I'm a defense attorney."

"Really? How interesting."

Madison stirred a little as she looked over her menu. "Do you find that difficult? Joe's told me about some of the cases. I couldn't imagine."

"It's not easy." Actually, for her it was quite easy. She could find loopholes and questionable evidence just about anywhere. It was why she was so good. The hours were long and it could be stressful, but finding a way for a good defense for her client was rarely difficult for her. It was just all about what the judge would allow and the jury would believe. A crap shoot of sorts.

"I bet not."

The waiter arrived and Rob encouraged Madison to order the wine. "Madison is a wine lover," he explained.

"And collector," Juan added. "Right?"

Rob nodded.

"Really?" Grace was a bit surprised. She would never peg Madison as someone who would be into wine. Then again, she would've never imagined her looking so well put together either.

"She has very fine taste," Rob said. "You'd be surprised." He smiled like he'd read her mind.

"I think we'll go with the Beaulieu Vineyard Red Blend," Madison said, handing the waiter the wine menu.

"That's quite expensive," Juan said, appearing concerned.

"Madison and I got it," Rob said. "Trust me. It will be worth it."

"Oh, so you're buying?" Juan teased. "When was this arranged?"

Rob smiled. "Earlier."

"Please. Sounds like Grace and I need to have a chat of our own," Juan said.

"Sounds like it," Grace agreed. "Maybe we should get dinner and let them get the wine."

"No, no, no." Madison said. "You two aren't allowed to make deals tonight. This is our treat."

"That's right," Rob said. "It got both Madison and I up off our rumps and out, so the thank you is ours."

"It got me up off my rump as well," Grace said.

"You don't date much, Grace?" Juan asked. "I find that hard to believe."

"Yes, so do I," Madison added, her eyes flickering with mischief.

Grace eyed her in return and grinned. "Yes, you would find that hard to believe, wouldn't you, Ms. Clark?"

Rob laughed softly.

Juan looked from one to the other, totally lost. "What am I missing?"

"Oh, so you know about the mark?" She pointed the question to Rob, who flushed.

Juan was desperate. "What mark? What am I missing?"

Grace decided to enlighten them all and lay the whole thing on the table. "The other day I had a hickey." She looked to Madison, who was very serious all of a sudden. "Right here." She brushed her hand over the cutout of the dress. "I had on a blouse in which you could see it, and Madison here obviously did."

The table was very quiet.

"I assumed that she'd made her own assumptions about it, so I sort of confronted her on it."

After a long silence, Juan said, "I see."

"But," Grace smiled, "it was just a one-time thing, and it was a mistake. Not something I normally do."

"Well," Juan said, "you're single, so you shouldn't worry about having to explain. Should you?"

"No, I didn't think so, but I apparently felt like I should."

"Why?" He grinned and rested his chin on his hands.

"Because I don't want Madison to think I sleep around when I have Jake to care for. I'm not like that. He does and always will come first."

Madison blinked. "You don't have to explain on my account."

"Yes, I do."

"Is that the only reason you want her to know that?" Rob asked. "Because of Jake?"

Now Grace flushed, and she was just about to try to explain her way out of answering when the waiter brought their wine. Madison stared at her as he opened the bottle and poured them each a glass. Grace didn't bother swirling or inhaling the aroma. She just took a large gulp and looked away from Madison's penetrating gaze.

"So tell me about Jake," Juan said, saving her ass.

"He's a good kid," Rob said with a smile. "Gonna make one hell of a rugby player."

"Yes, he did mention something about rugby the other day," Grace said.

"Rob's the coach," Madison said, having to clear her throat. "He's a great coach. The boys love him."

"Jake would make a wonderful addition. He's fast, from what I hear. And he has tenacity," Rob said.

"He does have that," Grace said with a chuckle. She looked to Juan. "My nephew is quite the character."

"Sounds like it." He grinned.

"He's coming around," Madison said.

"In fact," Rob said, "Madison said he may have a gift with horses."

Madison shot him a look, but Rob was focused on Grace.

"She also said that about you," he added.

Grace could feel Madison's entire body constrict. Even her jaw clenched, and red brushed her cheeks.

"Rob," Madison said.

"What? Tell her. It's great news. Very special." He smiled.

"Tell me what?" Grace was confused and a little alarmed. She didn't like the fact that they all seemed to know something about Jake while she didn't.

After a long glare at Rob, Madison finally looked to Grace. "Jake calms the horses."

She shook her head, still not totally following. "How?"

Madison spoke softly. "With just his presence."

"Oh." Grace couldn't help but smile. "Really?"

"Yes, he's very good with them. Puts them at ease. Especially Draco."

"The one who bucked him?"

"Yes."

Rob chuckled and Juan whispered, "Oh my God."

"There's no way Draco would've let anyone else climb on him. No way," Madison explained.

"And that's good?" Grace didn't like imagining Jake with the wild horse.

"It can be."

"Tell her what Marv said about her," Rob said.

Madison sighed. "Why don't you?"

They were like brother and sister bantering. She and Juan couldn't help but laugh.

"Don't mind if I do. Grace, Marv said he thought you had something special too. He saw it when you were working with that colt."

Grace wasn't sure what to say.

"You were good with the colt," Madison said. "You relaxed him."

"Do you like animals, Grace?" Juan asked.

"Yes."

"Really?" Madison asked.

"Yes, of course I do. I love them, in fact."

Madison seemed truly surprised.

"What about you, Juan?" Grace asked.

"Oh, yes. Especially horses. They are just so soulful, you know?"

"Yes, I know," Grace said softly.

"I didn't know that," Rob said, looking at Juan. "We'll have to go out to the ranch after dinner and show you around."

Madison leaned forward and took several hearty sips of her wine.

"Right, Madness?" he asked, pointing his gaze at her.

"Sure." She lowered her glass but avoided looking at Grace.

Grace considered protesting, but she really didn't want to. Going to the ranch with the three of them would be fun, and it would give her ample time to keep viewing Madison in a different light, even if it made them both a little edgy. She just couldn't bear to tear her eyes away from her.

Maybe I should protest. I told May I wouldn't be late, and then there's Jake.

But the waiter returned and took their orders before she could say anything. They all ordered steak, Madison a filet mignon. She said it went very well with the wine, and Grace knew just about any cut would. The wine was spectacular, and the more she drank, the more she liked it and the more she liked her company. Especially Madison, who looked so scrumptious sitting there in her white blazer with the open throat, bead necklace resting on her bare skin. Grace watched her sip her wine, watched her talk, watched her concentrate on Rob and Juan. She would do this by sipping from her own glass and looking over the rim carefully at Madison. A few times she caught Madison looking at her too, at which she would either glance away quickly or meet her gaze with a smile. Madison always returned the smile with a small polite one of her own. And once, it even lingered, and Grace swore she caught her staring at the cutouts of her dress that revealed a hint of cleavage.

Maybe she's just looking for the mark. Maybe I'm crazy.

Was there something going on?

"Maybe it's the wine," she said aloud before she realized it.

All three stared at her.

"Sorry?" Madison said.

"Oh, nothing. I—I sometimes talk to myself." She palmed her forehead. *I'm such an idiot!* "Would you please excuse me?" She rose and headed for the restroom, chastising herself the entire way. Luckily, the restroom was empty, so when she found a stall she called May, who answered on the first ring.

"Matchmaker."

"Matchmaker my ass!" Grace said loudly and then lowered her voice.

"Oh, so it's going well?"

"You set me up with Madison Clark!" she whispered.

"Who?"

"The—"

"The ranch lady?"

"Yes!"

"Oh my God. How—that's impossible! I didn't set you up with a cowgirl."

"Child psychologist, owns her own business. Sound familiar?"

"Oh my God."

"Can't you say anything else?"

"Not at the moment. So it's going terribly?"

Grace paused. "Not exactly. It's not—"

"Oh my God! You like her!"

"Shut up! I didn't say that."

She heard the main door open and close. "I gotta go." She ended the call and came out from the stall. Madison was standing there with one hand in her jeans pocket.

"Calling a friend to tell her about your hellish blind date?" She smirked, and Grace would have been offended if it wasn't so damn sexy.

"Of course not."

"Uh-huh. I don't blame you really. This wasn't what I had in mind either."

"What, me?"

"It was quite a shock."

"So I'm not the only one?" Her voice shook a little.

"In shock? No."

"Good." She ran her hand nervously through her hair.

"But I was hoping we could at least have a nice evening." Madison offered a smile.

"We are, aren't we?" Grace returned the smile and tried to allow the silkiness of her own hair to ground her. She dropped her hand when it didn't help.

"I am. But I get the feeling you might not be."

"Oh. No, I'm fine. I just—"

"Because if you want to go, I've thought about it and I

understand. And what Rob said about the ranch, you don't have to come."

"I don't know what to say."

"Just say what you want. I don't think you've had that problem before." She smiled again, ever so slightly, to show she was playing.

"I guess I haven't, have I?"

"Not exactly."

"Okay, then." She took a big breath. "I would like to stay for dinner and go to the ranch afterward."

Madison seemed to sway back a little in surprise. Or maybe she imagined it. "Really?"

"Yes. Is that okay? You haven't said how you feel about it."

"I'm good. That sounds good. I'm glad we're on the same page."

"Yes, it's nice. For a change," Grace said softly.

"Yes, it is," Madison said.

They looked at each other in silence for several moments. Grace wasn't sure what to say or what to do. If she spoke, it would surely give away the fact that her heart was pounding and her blood boiling in excitement just beneath her skin. If she moved, it would surely startle Madison and she'd fly away, like the rarest of butterflies never to return again, ruining the beautifully charged moment between them.

No, all she wanted to do was remain like this in this moment. Perfectly still. With Madison Clark standing across from her, fueling her fire with that intense and certainly soon to be fleeting look.

"You look very nice tonight," Madison said, the strain in her voice obvious.

Grace swallowed. "So do you."

"You didn't think I could clean up this nice, did you?"

Grace considered lying but she knew there'd be no use. She shook her head. "No."

"I didn't think so."

"I've made a lot of assumptions about you, Madison."

"And I you." She took a step closer. Grace didn't move.

"I'm sorry about that," Grace whispered.

Another step. "Are you?"

"Yes." Grace fought for the control she was desperately losing. Madison was inching closer, her gorgeous face looming. So close Grace could smell her tantalizingly clean-smelling cologne. "Are you sorry for the assumptions you've made about me?"

Grace reached out for her hand. She found it hot and smooth, slightly coarse at the base of her fingers. It sent her heart flying as if the hand had stroked the walls of her heart itself.

"I don't know."

"You don't know?"

"I'm not sure they're wrong."

Madison was an inch away and staring into her eyes.

Grace tilted her head slightly, wanting to inhale her breath. But Madison leaned in and bypassed her mouth to whisper in her ear.

"I refuse to kiss you in a public restroom."

Grace shuddered at the hot feel of her in her ear. She clung to her for support and nearly groaned at the strength she felt against her.

"I wish you would," she whispered back, finding her ear and inhaling her scent.

"No. Not here." She backed away and Grace nearly fell.

"Where, then?"

Madison tugged on her hand. "We have dinner to attend to."

Grace was flustered, terribly so. "Give me a moment?"

Madison nodded. "I'll be at the table."

Grace watched her go and then approached the sinks. Her skin was crimson from her neck all the way down to the cutouts where her chest and cleavage peeked through her dress. She thought about rinsing her face with cool water, but she didn't want to ruin her makeup. Instead, she concentrated on her breathing and on doing her hair. Her body was tingling from head to toe, and she kept going over what had happened.

Madison wanted to kiss her. Had indeed almost kissed her.

And then she'd come back with "where, then?"

"Ugh, God. How suave." How desperate could she sound? She would have to try to hide it better. Madison had her quivering with just a whisper. How could this woman be doing this? How did she always seem so calm and in control? It was getting beyond maddening, but God, how incredible it had been. The intensity between them had been palpable, thick and heavy. And oh, how she'd wanted her to kiss her. She'd nearly wrapped her arms around her and taken her herself, wanting to feel her warm mouth on hers pressing and pulling. But thankfully Madison had stopped, and Grace would definitely have to weigh the kissing against the control. But she already had a pretty good idea which would win, and Madison Clark would be the one standing while she lay crumpled in a combusted pile at her feet.

"Get a grip," she said as she exited the restroom.

Their food had arrived at the table, and all three gave her knowing smiles as she returned. Juan especially was grinning like a young schoolboy thrilled with a prank he just pulled.

"What?" she whispered to him.

"Oh, nothing."

She nudged him a little. "What's going on?"

He leaned in close to her. "You tell me."

"Nothing." She knew she looked aghast.

"Doesn't look like nothing. You both came out looking like you'd just run a mile and had loved every second."

"I look bad?" She touched her face and felt the heat that had remained.

"Not bad. But baaad. Know what I mean?"

She nudged him again. "Nothing happened."

"You two want to clue us in?" Rob asked.

"No," Grace said, a little too high in pitch.

Madison smirked and cut into her steak. Her eyes burned, but they were careful to avoid Grace.

"So you never did tell me about Jake," Juan said after chewing a small mouthful.

"I didn't?"

"Not really."

She sipped her wine. "He's sort of your average young teenager. He loves video games and music."

"What about girls?"

"No, thankfully, we aren't there yet. I don't think I could handle any more at the moment."

"How do you do it?" Rob asked. "Manage a home life with your job?"

"I—" She rested her fork. "I don't think I do it very well, to be honest. I try, God knows I try. But with my cases and Jake, sometimes I think I need to find a better way to balance it all."

The group grew silent. Then Madison spoke.

"I wish all my parents and guardians thought that way."

"Well, it's not easy for me to admit I'm inadequate."

"No one said you're inadequate," Madison clarified. "But thinking along the lines of improvement is huge. At least you're trying."

"Am I?" She looked at her. "Because it doesn't seem to be working."

"You are. And you're open to change, which is good. Really good."

"What would you suggest? For Jake's sake?" She really wanted to know. Needed to know. Because she was at a loss on how to make things better for him. The ranch was doing wonders, yes, but what about after that?

Madison shifted and looked to Rob. "I don't think I'm able to answer that, Grace."

"Why not? If not you, then who?"

"I don't know what your home life is like. All I know is what Jake has told me." She closed her mouth quickly as if regretting saying it, which caused Grace to react.

"What has he said?"

"I really can't say."

"Something bad?"

"No, nothing bad." Madison sighed and sipped her wine.

"Tell me."

"Grace."

"If it isn't bad, then tell me."

"He just said you're busy. With work."

"Oh." She stared at her plate, no longer hungry. "I knew that."

"Grace," Rob said. "You're doing a good job. You care. You're trying to be there for him. In my experience, which is a lot, I might add, those are two of the most important things a parent can do."

"I—I work too much, don't I?" She looked to Madison.

"I can't answer that."

"Of course not. Only Jake can." She wiped her mouth. "I should go."

"What? No," Juan encouraged her to sit. "Enjoy dinner. We're having fun."

"I should be at home with my nephew."

"But you're already here."

"Is he alone?" Madison asked.

"No. He's with my good friend."

"Then I'm sure he's fine. You should stay and enjoy dinner." She smiled at her softly. "Really."

"Stay and listen to us go on about rugby," Rob said. "If that doesn't entertain you, nothing will."

Grace tried to smile and found it catching. She took another sip of her wine and decided to try to relax. She didn't want to be rude, and Jake was probably just fine. Anyone would be with May. Besides, she hadn't said anything concerning when she'd called her.

Grace heated as she remembered Madison walking into the restroom. She hoped she hadn't heard anything. And yet somehow Madison had known she was calling someone to bitch about the date. Just how long had she been there? Did she really feel the same way? Both of them shocked and slightly repelled, yet truly attracted? What a strange way to feel about someone. But as she stared at Madison in the dim light of the restaurant, she knew that was exactly how they both felt. There was something there. Something powerful and just below the assumptions and first impressions.

The others moved on in conversation, but she found it difficult to concentrate. They were discussing how Rob and Juan met and how Rob thought Juan was cute but was afraid to ask him out because he didn't think he was good enough. They discussed assumptions and Grace felt herself warm again. She looked to Madison, who gave her a long, lingering look of interest as the men talked. As if to say, yes, we made our assumptions and now we're ready to move past them. How could this have happened so quickly? One chance evening and a brief encounter in a restroom, and almost everything had changed. To the point where she was ready to go to the ranch to see what might happen.

She reached for more wine but found her glass empty. Rob noticed, and as Madison offered to order another bottle, he shook his head.

"We'll have another at the ranch."

Madison glanced at Grace for her approval, then nodded. "Sounds good."

They sat for a moment after declining dessert. Juan made sure Grace would come to a rugby practice sometime. He winked, and as Madison and Rob took care of the bill he said, "Madison plays too. On the women's team."

"She does?"

"Mmm-hmm."

"She and Rob look so good all dirty and sweaty."

Grace cleared her throat, unsure what to say in response to the image he had just put in her head. "She's always dirty and sweaty."

He laughed. "Yes, but imagine her in a tight tee and short shorts."

"Oh." It did stir her, and she obviously couldn't hide it. Juan kept laughing. "I thought so. Come on, milady, let's blow this pop stand."

They rose and slowly headed for the door. Grace could feel Madison's eyes on her as she encouraged Grace to walk ahead of her. When they stepped outside, twilight was still lingering but the heat had diminished to a pleasant breeze. The parking lot lights had yet to come on and the evening air had a beautiful blue cast to it. Grace suddenly longed to take Madison's hand and go for a long walk in it. What would they talk about? What would they discuss? Would they laugh? Squeeze hands? Kiss?

"We'll meet you there," Juan said, giving Grace a nice kiss to the cheek. Rob did the same and waved, and she and Madison watched as they walked away, striding close to each other.

"They rode together," Grace said.

"Yes. Apparently, this wasn't their first date. Even though it was supposed to be."

"I thought they seemed rather chummy."

"Oh, they are." Madison placed her hand on the small of Grace's back as they moved through the parking lot. "I've never seen Rob so happy before."

"That's sweet."

"It is."

Grace wanted to lean into her, but they were at Madison's car before she knew it.

"This is you?" It was a midnight blue BMW, modern, high class, and very well cared for.

"Yes."

"Never would've pegged you for this."

"I didn't think so."

Grace tilted her head to look up at her. "You're just full of surprises."

Madison laughed. "So I've been told. Where are you?"

"Over there."

"Get in, I'll give you a lift."

"Thanks."

Grace climbed in and smelled the new leather and nearly rubbed herself against it. Every inch of it was shining and clean, and when Madison climbed in behind the wheel, Grace wanted to place her hand on her strong thigh as she shifted gears.

"You look good in this car," Grace said, meaning it.

"Thank you."

"No, really, you do. I can see how it suits you." *Not to mention how hot you look driving a machine like this. How hot would you look in my Mercedes?*

"I think it suits me. I love it. I also have another one at home. An older one I restored."

"Who would have thought?" Grace said. "Actually, I can definitely see you fixing up an old car."

"More my thing?" One side of her mouth lifted in a coy way.

"Yes."

"You're still assuming, Grace."

"So sue me. This is me." She closed her hand over Madison's and thanked her for the lift and for dinner. "Are you sure you want me to come to the ranch?"

"Of course. Why wouldn't I?"

"Yesterday you would've said no."

"Yesterday you would've killed me if I'd asked."

They both laughed.

"True."

"Okay, then come. I'll see you in a few."

"Okay."

"Bye, Grace."

"Bye."

Grace unlocked her car, slipped inside, lowered her vanity mirror, and asked with a crazy smile, "What the hell are you doing, Grace Marie Hollings?"

CHAPTER FOURTEEN

"What the hell do you mean you have to go?" Madison asked into her cell phone. She'd just pulled into her garage when Rob called.

"I just got an emergency call. I'm sorry."

"Sorry? Grace is going to be here any second."

"So don't cancel on our part. Enjoy your time together. You two looked like you could use some alone time."

"Rob, I swear to God if you set this up—"

"I didn't. I really do have a call. But honestly, this is working out for the best. She's divine, Madness. Really. Not at all what I expected."

"Well, you haven't seen her all—"

"All what? Upset, cranky, uptight?"

"Well, yes."

"I've seen you that way, and trust me, it ain't always fun. So come on, enjoy her. Get to know her. I know you're drawn to her. She's drop-dead gorgeous, for one thing."

"She is beautiful."

"Madness, she's gorgeous. And she's bright. And she seems to really care about her nephew."

"I thought you had a call?"

"I do, I'm driving to it, Juan's coming with."

"Okay, so go. She's pulling up now."

"Okay, see you, Madness. Oh, and don't fuck it up!"

She hung up and slid the phone into her back pocket. Grace came to a stop closer to the garage and climbed out carefully. Darkness was settling in around them, making her blond hair contrast sharply with the night and with her dress. She was stunning.

"Don't tell me I beat the guys," she said with a smile.

Madison threw up her arms. "You did."

"Well, where are they?" She moved closer, walking slowly in her heels.

"Turns out…"

"They're not coming?"

She lowered her arms. "Nope."

"They planned this out, didn't they?"

"Probably."

"So they obviously want us to spend time together," Grace said, shaking her head in disbelief.

"I guess so." Madison shoved her hands into her pockets. "You can leave if you're uncomfortable."

"No, I'm okay. I mean, unless you want me to go."

Madison laughed. "Okay, let's stop this. You are staying."

"Okay, then."

"Would you like to come in for some wine?"

She saw Grace glance around and hesitate. "Actually, I was wondering if I could see that colt."

Madison smiled. "Really?"

Grace nodded.

"All righty." She held out her arm and Grace tucked her hand just inside it. She also slipped off her heels and walked the flagstone path to the barn barefoot. Madison could feel her warmth and smell her perfume. Both made her dizzy with excitement and desire. Who was this knockout walking next to her? This intelligent, caring, humorous woman walking with her in the moonlight with her high heels dangling from her hand? It certainly wasn't Grace Hollings, was it?

"What's his name?" Grace asked as they entered the barn and came to the first stall where the colt stumbled to his lanky feet.

"I haven't named him yet."

"Why not?"

"He hasn't chosen."

"Oh right," she said. "The cowboy mentioned something like that. Can I go in and pet him?"

Madison unlatched the door. "Barefoot?"

"I'll watch where I step."

Madison allowed her in, followed, and closed the door. The colt kicked a little in excitement and ran from side to side. But when Grace called him and held out her hands, he came at once up to her.

"Aww, he's so sweet," she whispered, holding his face and kissing his snout.

"Careful," Madison said, growing uneasy. "You don't want to hold them there or put your face that close because they can move their head suddenly and knock you."

Grace ignored her, kissing on him profusely.

"Grace," Madison said, stepping up to her. "Please be careful. I don't want you to get another bruise like the one on your knee."

"The one on my knee is fine, and I heard you." She smiled. "But look at his little face. I can't help it."

"Here." Madison gently eased Grace back. "You want to create a bubble." She drew a semicircle in the hay. "This is your bubble. And that's his."

"But I don't want to stay in my bubble," she said. "I want to love him."

Madison hoped Grace couldn't see the rush of heat that burned her neck and face. *I want to love him.* The way she'd said it and the way she'd looked. It nearly melted her.

She cleared her throat and continued. "And you want to pet them on their withers. Here," she said, taking Grace's hand and placing it just below his mane. "Right in here." She helped her stroke, and her own breathing grew quick and sporadic at their close proximity.

"Like this," Grace whispered, looking at her.

"Yes."

"I feel so far away."

"You aren't. You're close. You're very close."

Grace looked into her eyes. "But I want to be closer," she said.

"I need to be closer." She stepped into Madison and angled her head.

"But you can't get much closer," Madison said, her eyes threatening to flutter closed.

"I think I can." She dropped her shoes and tugged Madison in close. "Like this," she whispered just before placing a warm, long, wet kiss on her lips. Madison shuddered and groaned against her.

"Yes," Grace said. "Just like that." She fanned her pale lashes at her as they struggled for breath.

Madison could taste her still, and she licked her lips, wanting more. Never had a woman's kiss stirred her so, melting and then steeling her bones. She longed for that melting feeling again and she pulled her closer and held her tightly. "Again," she said staring into her irises. "And then again after that."

Grace tangled her hands in the base of her neck. "I refuse to kiss you again in the middle of a horse stall."

Madison laughed and lifted her with ease up into her arms. "Then we'll go someplace else."

Grace laughed and called out for her shoes.

"Damn it." Madison eased her down, grabbed her shoes, and closed the stall door. She killed the lights as they ran from the barn back to the house, Grace laughing all the way.

"This feels so good," she said, twirling by the patio door.

"What does?"

Grace stared up at the midnight blue sky. "This. All of this. You. This place. That sky. I just feel so…free. Free to be happy."

"You are free to be happy."

Grace lowered her arms and looked at her. "Not always. Yesterday I wasn't free to be happy. Yesterday I had to hide how I felt for you."

"You—hid—you've had feelings?"

"Yes, haven't you?" But she held up her hand. "Wait, no don't answer that. I don't think I can handle hearing that it was solely this black dress that changed your mind."

Madison laughed softly and took her hand to lead her inside. "It wasn't solely the dress, but I'll admit it does have a way."

"I knew it."

Madison closed the door behind them and switched on the lights to the front main room. She heard Grace pull in a surprised breath at getting her first glimpse of the house.

"This is…spectacular," she said softly. "So Southwestern but so tastefully done." She turned to look at her. "Did you do this?"

"Yes."

"All by yourself?"

"Yes."

"Madison, wow."

"You like it?"

"I love it. This is by far the nicest working ranch I've ever seen. It should be in magazines."

"It has been. In two, actually."

"Get out—seriously?"

"Seriously. And," Madison said as she set Grace's heels aside and approached her from behind, "I did have feelings for you before tonight."

"I love the color of the walls in here. They almost look suede. And the way they complement the couches and that corner arched fireplace—Wait, what?" She turned in to Madison's arms. "You did?"

"I was attracted to you."

"You were."

"Yes."

"You've got a great way of hiding it."

"So do you."

"Touché."

"You were just so damn—"

"Bitchy?" Grace covered Madison's mouth with her finger. "Don't agree or I'll have to punish you."

"What if I want the punishment?"

Grace groaned. "You really were into me?"

"I liked you, yes. Very much. But I couldn't figure you out."

"What changed?"

"You."

"Me?"

"Yes, I saw a softer side to you tonight. A vulnerable side. I saw Grace."

"And that did you in?"

"That and the dress."

"Ahem." A deep grumble came from near the kitchen and Grace jumped in Madison's arms.

Marv rounded the corner and into the light. Madison felt Grace pull away quickly.

"I'm sorry, ladies," he said, looking at the ground. "I came to find Maddy, and well, I thought she just went out for supper or something. I'll show myself out."

Madison hurried to him. "I didn't know you were coming," she whispered.

"I didn't either. I just got in the truck and came."

"Where the hell are you parked?"

"Out behind the barn. I brought in some extra Bermuda hay from my place."

Madison shook her head as she walked with him to the door.

"I'm so sorry, Marv. Stay, please stay. We can have wine and talk."

"Darlin', you got all the company you need." He grinned. "Go on back in there."

But she could tell he wasn't truly happy, and she knew why. Grace was Jake's guardian. Nothing more needed to be said. He seemed to read her thoughts as he stared into her eyes.

"Be careful," he said snuggling his cowboy hat on tight. "Night, Maddy."

She watched him go and then slowly closed the door.

Behind her, she heard Grace rustling. When she turned she found her slipping on her heels.

"Where are you going?" Madison asked, her stomach doing flips.

"I think I better go, don't you?"

"Why? Because of Marv?"

"Yes."

"He went home."

"Is he as embarrassed as I am?"

"He'll shake it off."

"Will he?" She didn't seem convinced.

"Yes."

"Because I don't think I can. I don't think I can shake any of this off."

"What do you mean?"

"I mean…my feelings. This. Us. It's intense and we have Jake to consider and—"

Madison leaned back against the door, defeated. "No. Please no. Don't go. It took me days, hours, minutes, a crazy number of insane seconds to admit my feelings for you. I finally admit it, let myself feel it, and you're going to go?"

"Madison, you know I'm right. What about Jake?"

"Yes, Jake. You are right. He comes first. But he won't always be under my care."

"He'll always be under mine."

"Yes."

"So here we are."

Madison moved from the door and reached back to open it.

"Do you think I want to go, Madison?"

"I'm not sure."

"You're wrong. I want more than anything to stay."

"You can't."

"Why not?"

"You just said you can't."

But Grace moved closer. And closer. Until she was a breath away. "I don't want to go," she said as she leaned in and kissed her. "I so don't want to go."

"Then don't go." Madison kissed her back, and it deepened with Grace tugging on her head and darting with her tongue.

"I won't." Another deep kiss. "I can't." Another one. "Oh God, I just need to feel you. Madison, please." Grace kissed her so hard Madison's head spun. Her lips tingled pleasurably as they pulled apart. "Just touch me," she said. "Feel me." Wildly, she inched up her skirt, took Madison's hand, and forced it down into her lace panties. "Feel me," she purred as her eyes began to roll back.

"Oh Jesus," Madison whispered, feeling at once her hot, slick folds. "Oh Jes—" But Grace cut her off with another powerful kiss. She moaned into Madison's mouth as Madison's hand worked her, gliding up and down over her clit. "This is why I don't want to go. This is how you make me feel. Do you understand?"

"Yes."

"Do you feel the same? All wet and slick? For me?"

"Ye-es."

"Mmm. I'm gonna come. Oh God, I'm gonna come. No. Wait." She stilled Madison's hand and then unbuttoned Madison' s blazer. "I want to touch you," she said, her pupils widening as she stared at her white lace bra and slipped the blazer off her. "You're incredible," she whispered, stroking her abdomen up to her chest, causing Madison to quiver. "So powerful and strong."

"I want to take you," Madison said, wanting nothing more than to pick her up and carry her off to ravish her.

"You could too, couldn't you?" She continued touching her abdomen and then her arms. "You could completely have your way with me."

"Yes."

"And you would like that?"

"Oh, yes."

Grace shuddered and her eyes glistened. "I'd like that too. But first, let me touch you." She unbuttoned her jeans and slid her hand down the front. Madison hissed as Grace found her already soaking wet.

"Yees," Grace purred.

Madison slipped her hand back inside Grace's panties. They stroked each other and kissed and moaned.

"God, you feel good," Grace said, sucking on her neck and then attaching to her breast through her bra.

"Ah," Madison called out. "Mmm, Grace."

"Yes?"

Grace stopped. "Don't come."

"I'm close."

"Me too. Wait. Wa—"

And then she kissed her hard on the mouth and they stroked wildly, milking each other for the impending orgasm they were about to share.

"Now," Grace said and kissed her again and they both blew into bliss, tongues slipping and sliding along with their hands. Madison lost herself and cried out, having to pull Grace's head away to do so.

"Yes," Grace said again and again, watching her first with wild but then with heavy-lidded eyes. "Yes."

The sweet warmth in Madison's center pulsed against Grace's slender fingers as they rested. Madison could feel Grace's flesh pounding beneath hers. Touching her was better than she ever could've imagined. Feeling her next to her, on her, inhaling her scent, it was all far better than what heaven must be. And looking into her eyes, now, after they'd both climaxed was like looking into warm, liquid gold.

"You are the most beautiful thing I've ever seen," Madison whispered.

Grace blinked. "Madison," she said. "You are. Right at this moment." She touched her face. "Look at you."

But Grace's touch felt like fire itself, and the feel of her breath on her face fueled Madison all the more. Swiftly, she removed their hands and swept Grace off her feet. She carried her to the couch and set her down.

Grace smiled at her. "What do you have in mind, Madness?" she laughed softly. "I like that little nickname."

"You should. It means I'm crazy."

"Crazy about me?"

"Yes."

"Then I love it."

Madison laughed and leaned in to kiss her. It grew quickly and became hungry and fierce. Madison eased her back on the cushions when she tried to come forward. Then she pushed up her dress and spread her legs.

"Stay," she said when Grace tried to lift up. She pressed her down with one hand and lifted a leg over her shoulder with the other.

"My God, you're strong," Grace said, still trying to move.

"Yes, so don't try to move."

Grace laughed. "I can't help it. I'm turned on. I want to watch you."

"You can see just fine. She knelt and rubbed her face in her panties. She heard Grace inhale sharply.

"Mmm, so good," she said, sneaking out her tongue to rim the edges. She moved her face, tugging the panties to the side with her teeth. Grace's fingers came and held them to the side for her. It only turned Madison on more and she plunged her tongue into her flesh and licked her hard and heavy, up and down.

"Oh, fuck!" Grace cried out. "Oh God, Jesus, fuck."

Madison gave her more. And more. And then she took her clit and sucked as Grace spread her legs wider.

"Madison!" she cried. "Oh God, Madison."

Madison moved her head from side to side, taking her in further. She took more of her flesh in and sucked her off, using her tongue to stroke as she did so. Grace continued to cry out. Louder and louder. Her leg tightened on Madison's shoulder. Her body writhed. And she tasted and felt so damn good Madison never wanted to let her go. She wanted to die right there between her legs, making her—

Grace came then, spastic and loud and rough and crazy. Nearly tearing Madison's hair from her head with wild fingers. She pushed and bucked and slithered like a snake. Madison held on, so turned on she came against the seam in her jeans.

"Madison," she gasped, coming down. "Madison."

Madison held firm and then released the pressure slowly, licking her softly until she was pulling away. Her own face was hot and tingling, as was her crotch. She collapsed onto Grace's leg and nibbled her thigh while relishing her scent and taste.

She was about to suggest they go into the bedroom when Grace's phone rang.

"Oh shit."

Grace fumbled for her purse, which had been deposited on the couch earlier. Madison eased off her and saw her face contort with worry. "It's home." She flipped open the phone. "Hello?"

She still sounded breathless and she yanked her dress down as if whoever was calling could see. She even crossed her legs.

"Really? That's great." She smiled. "Okay." She stood. "When? Oh, I don't know. Now? Well, I don't know, Jake." She fingered her forehead. "I'll see. Uh-huh. Okay. Bye." She closed the phone and looked over at Madison, who still kneeled on the floor.

"You have to go," Madison said.

"I don't have to."

"But you should."

Grace chewed her lower lip. "I can call back and tell him I'll be a while."

"No, don't."

"My friend May will understand. And Jake—Jake's just excited about a movie she brought over."

Madison stood. "You should go. He needs you."

"He's watching a movie, Madison." She moved toward her, touched her face. "He'll be fine."

"No, he needs you. Now more than ever. It's times like this when he really wants your attention."

Grace pulled away. "What are you saying? You'd rather me go watch a movie than be with you?"

"If it means spending time with Jake, then yes."

"Jake." She dropped her hand dramatically. "So I'm not doing right by Jake. We're back to that."

"I never said you weren't doing right. But he does need attention."

"He gets plenty of attention."

"He needs it from you."

Grace gathered her purse, obviously upset. "I guess I better go, then."

"Grace, wait. Don't leave mad."

"I won't, then. I'll just leave."

Her face had that pinched look to it. The one she usually wore when at the ranch. And just like night and day, the sun had risen and the old Grace was back. Stubborn, angry, temperamental. Madison wondered if it was possible to penetrate that barricade or if it was something that just had to dissipate on its own.

"Grace," Madison called out to her as she stumbled barefoot to her car. "Grace, wait. I didn't mean anything by it."

"I'm not a fit parent, this I already know. I don't need you rubbing it in with your calm suggestions." Grace opened her car door and tossed her purse and shoes inside. "Do you know that I rarely take time for myself? That all I do is work and worry about Jake? Tonight…this…was special. It meant something. I *felt* something."

"So did I." But she stopped when Grace shook her head.

"I don't know if you did or not. But I can't worry about that. You brought the perspective back to me, and now I need to go home." She climbed inside and started the car. Madison saw her wipe away a tear as she put the car in reverse.

The dust behind her tires looked pink from her taillights as she sped away. And Madison was left whispering in the darkness.

"Grace."

❖

The next morning brought nothing but gray light. Gone was the usual pale blue, the breaking of a new beautiful day. All that remained was a dingy dawn, a leftover stain from the night before. Madison sat festering in it as it seeped through the windows, an empty wine tumbler dangling in her hand and an old jazz record playing again and again. She'd tried to drink the night away, to drink Grace and her hot mouth away, but it hadn't worked. It had only soaked the memories, made them sweeter, made them replay and resaturate.

And Billie Holiday hadn't helped either. Crooning like only she could, talking about things that seemed to emulate every nerve ending in Madison's body. Making her yearn, burn, cry out, and tear up.

Should she call?

Should she not?

Should she forget her?

How in the hell could she?

And more wine had come, splashing into her tumbler, asking her how in the hell it had happened in the first place. A question she could not answer. A snake that had hidden in plain sight with wild, beautiful colors had somehow reached up and bit her. A wild, beautiful creature in plain sight. Right there in front of her. Warning her of its danger but seducing her with its colors.

Grace is not a snake.

Not in the literal sense. But she was beautiful, and she had snuck up on Madison and knocked her for a loop. And her bite, it felt deadly. Like if she didn't get the antidote soon she would indeed die.

"I need to call." She rose, convincing herself it was to check on Grace. But she stopped with cell phone in hand, debating. It was five a.m. on Sunday morning. Grace would be asleep. She would've long forgotten their encounter. Madison had already looked the fool in trying to encourage her in what do. She'd offended her and stuck her nose in where it didn't belong. Yes, she'd done enough damage.

She closed off the bottle of wine and replaced it in the cooler. Sleep called from the bedroom, and she purposely left the stereo on. Let Billie play. Let Billie sing. Let Billie soothe.

But it was another voice that came to her as she fell asleep. It was Grace, and she was calling out her name.

Chapter Fifteen

"Grace, it's been over a week. You need to talk to her," May said, sliding in next to her at the conference table in one of their larger rooms. "And you need to eat." She slid a salad in front of her, but Grace pushed it away, not in the mood for rabbit food.

"I don't know what to say, and I eat plenty."

"You say, hey, I'm sorry. I really like you and I want to jump your bones again. How hard is that?"

"I can't say that."

"Which part?"

"Any of it."

"Why not?"

"Because I already ruined everything just by starting something. I have too much to do. I have Jake, I have work." She'd avoided Madison for days, even sending Janine to get Jake. True, most of those days she was in court, but still.

"You have fear," May continued for her. She opened the salad, along with her own, and squirted on the packaged dressing.

"It's not fear. It's practicality. She told me to go be with Jake."

"So she's not selfish, so what? She probably felt like an ass knowing you had to choose. She sounds like a stand-up gal to me."

"You wouldn't understand."

"No, of course not. I date gorillas, right? The harder of the species? I don't have a clue what it's like to be torn between a man and his kid."

"I didn't mean that."

"I know. You're just crabby. You've been getting no sleep and you look like hell."

"It's this case." Grace took a fork and picked at the salad. The conference room was quiet and sparse save for their notes and binders strewn about the long table. "I've never worked one I didn't feel good about."

"Don't tell me it's because he's guilty. We helped at least four guilty ones get off. You know it as well as I do. It's the game we play."

"It is because he's guilty."

May sighed. "Grace. Don't do this to yourself. This is our job. It's just a job." She grew concerned. "Why am I telling you this? You know this stuff. You usually say it to all the newbies. It's just a job."

"But it's not just a job. Not anymore." She grabbed a binder and flipped through it. "Look at this. Look at his priors. Four of them. Four!"

"So? He was young, and on the latest the arresting officer is questionable."

"No, you don't get it. If we get him off, he'll just do it again. Or maybe even something worse."

"We can't worry about that. We are just here to defend them to the best of our ability."

"No, May. I have to worry about that. I can't help it."

May sat back and pushed her salad away. "What's come over you?"

Grace sighed and rested her forehead in her hand. "I don't know."

"Are you okay?"

"No, I don't think I am."

"Is it Madison?"

"No. She has nothing to do with this."

"Then what is it?"

"I don't know. I just know that when I'm up late working on this case, I no longer feel right about it. I don't want to excuse this man's behavior again. I don't want to enable him to keep ruining others' lives. And he may escalate, May. The next house he breaks into or the next woman he steals from, he may use a weapon. He tried to use force on that arresting officer."

"That's bunk. The officer roughed him up. It was self-defense. We have the video to prove it."

"You sound like an attorney!"

"Because I am."

"Can you talk to me as just May? As just an average, everyday citizen?"

"Fine. Okay."

"What about the peeping Tom? Our last guy?"

"Ugh, him."

"Yeah, what if he escalates like the prosecution said he might? To assault or even rape or murder? He'd already broken into a woman's home. And I don't care who he was. Doctor or Joe Schmoe. He has issues!"

"What if? Grace, we can't control the world."

"No, but we can help it. That man needed help. He didn't need to walk out of court scot-free to go do it again."

"So what are you saying here? You want to switch teams?"

"I don't know what I'm saying. I just know I'm tired. And that having Jake has made me take a hard look at things."

"I see," May said softly.

"Do you realize if Jake didn't get help, he'd end up sitting across from us one day, knee-deep in charges?"

"You don't know that—"

"Yes, I do, May. I do. And if my sister lived in this state she would've been a client as well. And that's not okay with me."

They were silent for a long moment. Then May spoke. "Sounds like you have a lot of thinking to do."

"Yes."

"Are you still going to work on the case?"

"Of course."

"Think we can win it?"

"I don't know. But I'll give it my best."

"Are you sure?"

"Yes, May. My job, for the time being, is still number one."

"Phew." She laughed nervously.

"But I don't think it always will be."

Chapter Sixteen

"My chores are done," Jake said, jogging up to Madison. "What can I do now?"

Madison grunted as she shoved a full wheelbarrow up a small mountain of manure to dump it, adding to the growing pile. Jake stood alongside her, completely at ease with being ankle-deep in manure.

"Your boots are getting dirty," she said, easing the wheelbarrow back into a stand. She wiped the sweat from her brow as he looked down.

He shrugged. "So?"

"So?" She turned to wheel the cart back to the pens where another load was surely needed. "If I recall, you recently had a fit about getting crap on your shoes."

He walked with her, trying to keep up with her long strides, something he did every day. "That wasn't recently. That was, like, days ago."

"You've changed your mind, then?"

He nodded. "I guess. It doesn't bother me so much now."

"It shouldn't," she said. "Considering you shovel it every day."

"That doesn't really bother me either. But I still want better chores. What else can I do today?"

"You've been in an eager mood lately," she said, grinning.

"I just want to help out. Do what you do."

"Why's that?"

"I don't know. It makes me feel good, I guess." He seemed shy all of sudden, as if realizing just how helpful he'd become.

"It isn't cool, you know," she said, laughing. "Doing everything I do."

He squinted over at her. "Yes, it is. It is to me. You know how to do, like, everything."

"Well, thanks."

He looked away, obviously embarrassed. "I just like to learn."

She returned the cart to the pen, released it, and clapped him on the shoulder. "That's the best thing you've said yet, Jake. Now let's see how these two are doing." Pulling the gloves from her hands, she eyed the two boys who were walking around shoveling manure.

They'd been arguing earlier over money. Because they lived in a group home together and were only allowed so much spending money a month, this seemed to be a common theme for trouble between them. Apparently, Alex had already spent his allotted amount, and he wanted J.J. to share his. Lack of money and arguing over what they couldn't have, she mused, was most likely why they ended up shoplifting in the first place.

"Alex, be sure you're helping J.J. out," Madison said, noticing the difference in work amount. J.J. was doing nearly all of the shoveling while Alex merely walked around and poked with his shovel.

"Yeah, I'm doing everything," J.J. said.

At hearing that, Alex turned and in a split second, his face twisted with rage and he charged at J.J.

Madison lunged forward with two giant strides and caught him with the full force of her body. He continued to push as if she weren't there, yelling at J.J.

Madison braced herself for the impact of J.J., but it didn't come. She could hear him scurrying, hear him yelling in return, but he didn't come. Turning, she braced her arms around Alex and caught sight of J.J. struggling in Jake's grasp. Jake was in front of him, holding him by the shoulders, trying to talk him down.

"It's not worth it," Jake yelled. "J.J., listen. It's not worth it.

You'll have to run and you'll have to shovel crap forever." He shook him. "You'll have to run!"

J.J. stilled while Alex kept yelling. Madison squeezed him harder and backed him up. When she had him a safe distance away he finally calmed and went limp.

"You done?" she asked, forcing him to look in her eyes.

He nodded.

"What?" she asked.

"Yes, ma'am."

"Good." She released him but stood between him and J.J. "You go work in that corner and cool down. We'll talk after that."

"Yes, ma'am." He picked up his shovel and kicked it as he walked.

Madison watched him for a while before heading back to J.J. To her surprise, Jake was shoveling too, encouraging J.J. along the way.

"If I help you, you guys will get done faster," Jake said. "And then the crap chore will be done." He worked as best he could with his hurt wrist, which was no longer splinted. And J.J. worked with him, the pair making a good team.

Madison shook her head in pleased disbelief and crossed to the gate where Marv had come to a stand.

"Remember that kid you called hardheaded and spoiled?" she asked with a grin.

"Yeah."

"Well, that's him." She nodded toward Jake, who now had J.J. laughing as they worked. "What do you think now?"

He scratched his five o'clock shadow. "I'd say he's coming along."

"Coming along? He's done his chores the past few days without any trouble. He does extra chores eagerly. And now he's breaking up arguments and helping the others. He's like a different kid altogether."

"We've seen it happen before," he said. "Like a light switch goes off."

She couldn't help but grin. "I know, but with this kid it feels really good."

"That because of his aunt?"

Madison gripped the back of her neck, knowing it was an honest question. "No. I'm just real happy for him. I knew he had it in him."

"What about his aunt? Does she know?"

"I left her a message this morning. I'll leave her another one tonight."

"She won't talk to you, huh? I tried to warn you." He breathed deeply and tried to make eye contact with her.

"I better go talk to Alex." She turned and left him there, leaving his question along with him. Grace wouldn't talk to her, but that was going to change. It just had to.

CHAPTER SEVENTEEN

Grace deleted the last message from her phone as she pulled into the garage. Madison had called several times to say how well Jake had been doing at the ranch. He'd been doing as he was told and even doing chores that weren't asked of him. And he'd helped to break up an argument. He'd been doing well, and she'd suspected as much since all he'd done was talk about Madison and the ranch and all the different things they did each day. It was all he wanted to talk about. Ms. Clark this, Ms. Clark that.

And he was even acting differently at home. He was getting up on time, making his bed, insisting on doing his laundry. He was saying yes, ma'am, no, ma'am, using Madison's tone of voice when he spoke. It reminded her so much of Madison she had to walk away sometimes. It was hard enough not to think of her without Jake walking around emulating her all the time. While his behavior was a welcome change, it unnerved her all the same.

She just couldn't seem to shake Madison Clark.

After killing her engine, she exited the Mercedes, closed the garage door, and walked inside the house. The first thing she noticed was the smell of something cooking, something like garlic and tomato sauce. The second thing she noticed was the darkness, save for a small lamp in the corner of the living room.

Jake was sitting there on the couch with his head slumped. When he raised it and she saw his face, she nearly dropped her briefcase.

"What? What's wrong?"

He didn't speak for a moment. Then, "Happy freaking birthday."

She blinked in confusion. And then she remembered. He'd wanted to have dinner with her.

"Oh God, Jake, I'm so sorry. I totally forgot." This time she dropped her briefcase and came forward. She tried to touch him, but he jumped up and hurried to the kitchen.

"Forgot? Forgot?" he yelled, switching on the lights. "That's worse than saying you have to work, Aunt Grace." He held up plates full of spaghetti. "I made you dinner. I *made* you dinner. A homemade recipe I got online. I did this for you." His voice caved as emotion came over him. "But no. You forgot, you're three hours late, and again I'm all alone in this goddamn house."

"Jake, I'm so sorry. So very sorry." She crossed the room and tried to stand next to him, but he moved. She just wanted to hug him so badly.

"Sorry sucks, Aunt Grace. You said you would be here. Who works late on their birthday?"

I do. I always have. God, how could I have forgotten?

"I just—I'm not used to even celebrating my birthday."

He walked to the kitchen table, clanked down her full plate, slumped into a chair, and tossed her a gift.

"Open it," he said.

She sat across from him, heart hammering. She'd never seen him so hurt before. It was tearing at her. "Aren't you going to eat?"

"I'm not hungry," he said, glaring at her.

With her hands fumbling, she managed to open the small gift. It was a nice ballpoint pen set, heavy and shiny, nestled in a large velvet box.

"I thought you could use it for work. Since that's all you do," he said with sarcasm.

"Jake, where did you get this?" She was moved.

"Online. I used one of my gift cards."

She covered her mouth, trying not to cry, and then rose to hug him. He stiffened beneath her like always, so she squeezed him harder.

"Thank you. This means a lot to me. That you would even think to do this."

He pushed her away and rose as well. "Yeah, well, it's more than you do. You don't think about me."

She shook her head. "Jake, I…Yes, I do. All the time."

"No, you don't. You think about work. That's it. I wish—I wish I lived with Ms. Clark."

Grace stepped back, shocked and hurt. "Don't say that."

"I do!" Tears formed in his eyes. "She wouldn't forget. She would care. She *does* care!"

Grace fought her own tears. "I'm tired of hearing about Ms. Clark!"

"Well, I'm tired of your bullshit!"

"Then you just continue to hang out with Ms. Clark if that's what makes you happy. I'm sorry I'm not perfect like her!"

"I will!" He shoved the plate of spaghetti to the floor and ran down the hall to his room, where he slammed the door.

She followed quickly and found the door locked. "Jake!" She knocked hard.

"Go away!"

"Jake, please."

"Leave me alone, Aunt Grace. You're good at that."

"Jake." She rested her forehead against his door.

His stereo came on, drowning her out.

Grace left his room and returned to the kitchen. As she knelt and began picking up the plate and the food, hot tears fell, along with confusion and a profound sense of loss.

❖

Grace drove toward the setting sun, contemplating her next move. Had she said too much? Was she just overwhelmed? She wasn't sure anymore. She wasn't sure of anything. And right now she was late for Jake's rugby practice. She'd promised to be there at six, but work had needed her attention, and honestly, she wasn't looking forward to sitting through this practice. She knew zip about rugby, it was starting to get hotter out, and she really didn't want to run into Madison.

Avoiding her had been easy. Trying not to think about her, though, not so much. She didn't know what to say. What to do. Jake already worshipped her while Grace was struggling to do her best just to keep him talking to her. It was like nothing was good enough. She wasn't Madison, she didn't have all the time in the world, and she wasn't Gabby. She was just Aunt Grace, and that wasn't cutting it. Allowing Jake to ride with Madison to practice had been huge, which seemed to really surprise Madison. But she felt like she was losing him. His behavior had changed, yes. Significantly so. But it was like living with a man now. A grown man obsessed with his job, leaving no room for her.

She pulled up at the park and cut her engine, wishing she could kill her mind. But the thoughts kept coming. Jake was changing and she wasn't. That left things between them strained. He might as well be living on another planet.

After crawling from the car, she removed her blazer and clutched a small bottle of water. She made her way to the fields and found a spot on the stands. Around her, dozens of boys ran. She found Jake right away, running near the front, his splint gone. She wondered when and why he'd taken it off.

"Hi," Madison said, coming up on the stands to sit next to her.

Grace felt her mouth fall open and she forced herself to look away. Madison was wearing short shorts and a sports bra. Sweat coated her muscular body.

"Hello."

"I finally got you cornered." Madison smiled softly and sipped from her own bottle of water.

"Thanks for giving Jake a ride." It was the only safe thing she could think to say.

"No problem. Thanks for letting him come. He's going to love this."

"I'm sure he will. He loves everything else you two do together."

Madison grew quiet. “Are you okay?”

Grace met her eyes. “Don’t I look okay?”

“Honestly, no. You look…tired.”

“Tired? Ha. Who’s tired? I haven’t got time to be tired.”

Madison touched her hand. “Really, Grace, you do.”

“Well, thanks. You look sweaty. Hot and sweaty. And gorgeous.”

Madison’s grip tightened. “So do you. You always do.”

“But tired came to your mind first. Guess I must be a sight.” She knew she was. Her eyes were red-rimmed with dark shadows beneath. Her skin was paler than usual.

“I’m just concerned.”

“No need to be.” She forced a smile. “I’m fine.” But she kept her hand still and wished Madison would move hers. She couldn’t think straight around her, and her touch was like fire itself.

“I want to see you. Please have dinner with me. You can bring Jake.”

“I can’t. I have work.”

“What about Saturday? Or Sunday?”

“I don’t think so. I’m really swamped right now.”

“Is everything okay? Jake said you’ve got a heck of a case.”

“I do.” She looked at her. “What else does he tell you? That I’m never around? That he gets no attention? That I suck as his guardian?”

Madison shifted to face her more. “No. Grace, what’s wrong?”

“I don’t know, you tell me. You know my nephew better than anyone.”

“So that’s what’s bothering you. Jake and me. I thought it might.”

“What’s that mean?”

“We’ve been spending a lot of time together.” Her eyes twinkled in the sunlight, but there was seriousness to them. “He’s come a long way in a short amount of time. I thought you’d be pleased.”

“I am in some ways. In other ways…he’s just a miniature you.”

Madison looked away. Then she stood. "I don't know what that means, but—"

Grace grabbed her hand. "Don't. Please. I'm sorry. I don't know what the hell's wrong with me."

Madison remained standing; her tight jaw showed she was still upset. "I hope you figure it out," she said. She gave Grace one last long look and headed back down the bleachers. Her strong back shimmered in the setting sun, and more than one head turned to look at her. Grace could still catch her scent. Her clean-smelling cologne mixed with the warmth of salty sweat. God, she looked good. She felt good, she sounded good.

What is wrong with me? I've probably just lost her forever now.

She buried her head in her hands. *Lost her? Did I ever really have her?*

"Hey, where's Ms. Clark?" It was Jake and he was panting. "I saw her up here."

"I don't know."

"Well, can she take me home? Coach Rob says we'll be here until the women are done. Says he needs to run our butts all night."

"I can come get you."

"Nah, I know you need to work, Aunt Grace." He pointed to her water. "Mind if I take this?"

"No, go ahead." She was surprised that he asked. Before he would've already downed it. His manners had greatly improved.

"I gotta go," he said trotting back down the stands. "It's time for burpees!"

"Burpees?"

"Ah yes, burpees." Juan slid in next to her. He gave her a hug and said, "Watch and learn."

Down on the field the boys lined up spread apart. They stood with hands at their sides, and when a whistle blew, down they went onto their chests. Another whistle and they were back up and jumping high in the air, arms raised.

"That's one burpee," Juan said.

"Wow." Down they went again at the next whistle. "I can't believe he likes this."

"Most boys do. I've always loved getting physical. Makes you feel incredible." He elbowed her playfully. "You should try it."

"Riiight."

"No, seriously. Look back there."

They turned and faced the women's field where they were lined up doing the same exercise.

"You could do it."

Grace stared in disbelief. There were at least twenty muscular women falling to the ground and pushing themselves back up. Most of them were wearing next to nothing.

"See Madison?" Juan asked, pointing.

"Oh, yes." She'd found her right away and homed in on her glistening body and well-etched muscles. "Oh, yes," she whispered, remembering what they felt like beneath her fingertips.

Juan put his arm around her and squeezed. "You really like her, don't you?"

"'Like' is not the right word," she said softly.

"More than that?"

She nodded. "So much more."

"Then what's stopping you?"

She turned to face the boys again. The burpees continued and Jake looked spent, his arm dangling. But to her surprise, he kept on.

"I suppose you know everything?" she asked, knowing Madison had probably told Rob, who'd probably told him.

"I know you won't talk to her."

"I just did."

"Well, why not before then? Didn't you two hit it off?"

"We did, yes."

"So—"

"I don't know what's wrong," she said, growing upset. "I can't answer that."

He squeezed her again. "Okay," he said. "Just know I'm here if you need me."

"Thanks."

"Sure thing. Want to learn a thing or two about rugby?"

She wiped away a tear and turned, needing to see her again. "Yes, but only if I can watch Madison."

Chapter Eighteen

I ain't gotta tell you to be careful," Marv said as they bathed one of their ponies.

"No, sir, you don't. Although actually you already have," Madison said.

"I'm just saying." He winked and laughed at himself. "Isn't that what the boys say?"

"Yes." She chuckled herself. "But please don't start saying 'epic' again or I'll have to kill you."

"Deal. Anyway." He began rinsing the soap from the pony, starting at her legs so she could get used to the temperature and the feel of the water. "Be careful there, Maddy, with that woman. She's just like the other two. All caught up in her career."

"Marv, really, I don't need to hear this."

"Well, now, yes, you do. I can see you moping around here day after damn day just because she won't talk to you. And, well, it's starting to piss me off. Who cares if she won't get out of her fancy car? It's her loss."

"Marv—"

"Honestly, you're better off. You were happier alone before she came along. Why are you so darned attracted to those types, Maddy?"

"First of all, she's not like the others. She's different."

"How?"

"Because she cares."

"About what?"

"Jake, the animals…"

"Her career. Hell, all that boy ever says is how much she works."

Madison almost cringed and looked around to make sure no one could hear, but it was Sunday and they were alone on the ranch.

"I just don't think she has that figured out yet."

"You're making excuses for her. Damn it, Maddy you're going to get hurt. Worse than you already have. You think I don't hear that loud music early in the morning? I know you're passed out on the couch, drinking her away."

She tossed a scraper to him rather hard. "Marv, don't."

"Just let her go."

"I can't."

"Why not?"

"Because I care about her and I care about Jake."

They began scraping the water off the pony. "What happens when Jake's gone?"

"I don't know."

"I'll tell you what. She leaves, he leaves, and you never see either one of them again."

"Maybe."

"And you'll be worse than you are now."

She kept scraping and then retrieved the mane and tail brushes. She didn't want to talk about this with him or with anyone, for that matter. Rob had already tried. She simply had nothing to say. Grace had her issues, and for whatever reason she wanted nothing to do with Madison. That fact was clear.

But it didn't mean she could just switch off her desire or feelings.

"I think I've been doing pretty good," she said aloud.

"No, you haven't."

She scoffed. Just because she was listening to her music and drinking her wine all night long didn't mean anything. She still did her job; she still helped Jake and the boys. Everything was fine. On the outside. And the rest nobody needed to know about.

"Can we change the subject?" she asked.

"Sure. Gladly." He grabbed a finishing brush and got to work on brushing the pony's face with the soft bristles.

"I need to ride out and check on the trail for the ride this coming weekend. You been out there lately?"

"Not in a while."

"I hope all is still well. Bobby said he thought there might be some coyote problems."

"Well, we'll have to go out every day, then, till they get chased off, I guess."

Every few months, depending upon the group and how well they did, Madison and Marv took the boys and their guardians on a trail ride out toward the mountain. She'd had picnic tables and shade built in years ago for such events, and the boys loved cooking out and tossing the rugby ball around.

This weekend promised to be a good one, and she couldn't be prouder of this group of boys. Tomorrow, they started riding individually to practice for the trail. Come Saturday, they'd be old pros and would love showing their guardians all there was to know about horses and riding. It helped to build confidence and pride when they got to teach. It instilled in them all the learning they'd done. It was a win-win situation, and she was very much looking forward to it.

"How about now?" Marv asked, finishing with the pony. They untied her and led her to her stall. "We could take those two fillies out and check the trail."

"Can't," she said, giving the pony one last rubdown.

"Got plans?"

"Actually, yes. I've got somewhere I need to be."

"Do I want to know where?"

"Probably not."

"Damn it, I was afraid you were gonna say that."

❖

An hour later, Madison pulled up to the amusement park and wove her way inside. The giant castle building was chock full of video games. Three stories held every game imaginable, and Madison could easily see why Jake had been so excited about coming. He'd invited her a few days ago and she'd put him off as best she could, unsure if she should accept. But he'd really insisted, and finally he'd let on that Grace wanted her to come too.

That had been enough to get Madison there, and it probably wouldn't take much to keep her there either. Grace's smiling face would be plenty of pay-off, despite the strong crowd of young teens weaving through game machines, laughing and shouting.

"This place is unreal," she said, taking in the open three-story structure.

"Yeah, and outside they have go-karts and roller coasters," Jake said, hopping up to her. "Come on!" He took her hand and shoved through the huge double doors to the outside. The warm air mingled with her skin, and the smell of soda pop and all things sticky entered her nose just before the smell of go-kart exhaust did.

"Where's your aunt?"

"She's around."

"Around?"

"Yeah, come on. Let's do the go-karts."

"Jake—I—"

"Jake?"

They turned and found Grace staring at them in disbelief.

"Hi," Madison said, feeling her discomfort.

"Uh, hi," Grace said. "Jake, what's going on?"

"Nothing. I just thought Madison might want to come too. She said she did," Jake said.

Madison heated. "You didn't know I was coming?"

"No." Grace shifted and gripped her soda cup harder.

"I'm sorry. I should go."

"No, no. Stay, please," Grace said. But her face showed her letdown. She wasn't happy to see Madison, not happy at all.

"I should really go," Madison said again, face heating in embarrassment.

Grace seemed to ignore her. "Jake, apologize to her."

"What for?" The pinched look was back, the one just like

Grace wore, and he shoved his hands into the pockets of his plaid skate shorts.

"For asking her to come," Grace said.

"So what if I did. I like her."

"That doesn't matter, Jake. You didn't tell me about it."

"So what? You would've said no. You say no to everything," Jake said, his voice showing his growing anger.

"I do not," Grace whispered.

"You do too."

"I just thought tonight was supposed to be for you and me. You know, to spend some time together."

"You've been on the phone since before we got here," he said.

Madison placed a hand on Jake's shoulder. "I'll see you tomorrow," she said softly.

"No, don't you go," Grace said to her. "I'll go." She started to walk away. "Bring him home at a decent time."

Madison took off after her, caught her by the elbow, and walked with her inside.

"You can't leave," Madison said. "Grace, please."

"Don't tell me what to do, Madison. You're the one who wanted me to spend some quality time with him. Well, I tried! Now you can have more time with him. It's what he wants anyway."

Madison tried to talk back, but it was so loud she could hardly think. She looked around and saw a photo booth. She pulled her inside and yanked the curtain shut.

"What are we doing in here?" Grace asked.

"I'm trying to talk to you."

Grace started to protest, but Madison grabbed her face.

"Tell me why you don't want me here," Madison insisted.

"Because I wanted to spend time with Jake." Grace looked hurt and serious and almost…lost.

"Why?" Madison asked.

"Because I love him and I feel like I'm losing him all over again."

"It's not because you don't want me?"

Grace grew silent. Then, "No."

"Then kiss me."

Madison leaned in and barely touched her lips. Grace let her but kept pulling back ever so slightly. Their breathing was quick and tight, around them the video game world spun. Grace came forward and kissed her lightly but pulled away again. They danced that way, just between kisses for a long, punishing eternity.

"Please," Madison whispered.

"I—"

Grace's cell phone rang and Madison groaned. "Can't you just throw that thing out? Just for the evening, can't you turn it off?"

Grace scowled and fumbled for it. "No, I can't," she answered with irritation in her voice. "Hold on a sec." Her hand covered the phone. "I have to go."

"This isn't right, Grace," Madison said, following her out of the booth.

"What isn't right, Madison? Him staying here with me when he'd rather be with you?"

"None of this is right."

But Grace turned and headed for the main door.

"None of this is right," Madison repeated.

❖

Grace cried the whole way home. What could she do? Jake was pulling away. She needed to work. The trial was winding down. This was just how things were. She was going to have to suck it up and get on with it.

At least Jake was out of trouble now. Yes, he hardly spoke to her anymore and the house felt cold and unlived in, but at least he was out of trouble. Madison was a great influence. She couldn't ask for a better one.

She even had her own desire to be with her. But that couldn't happen. Not with things like this. She couldn't allow herself to focus on Madison when Jake was pulling further away and work was keeping her up all hours of the night.

She just had to focus on the trial. She'd done her best with Jake. It was all she could do.

Her cell phone rang again and she eyed the number in the display. As if things couldn't get any worse. She fought tears again as she readied to answer.

Please, God, let it be good news.

But in her heart, she knew that it wasn't.

CHAPTER NINETEEN

Jake," Madison called as she trotted up to him. He was doing his chores on his own again. His slender arms were tanned and sinewy with new muscle, his face hard with seriousness.

"Yes, ma'am?"

"What's going on? You okay?"

He shrugged.

"You've been real quiet lately. Even the other boys have noticed."

"Just doing my chores," he said, his voice flat.

"Everything okay at home?"

"It's not my home, and yes."

"It's not your home? What's that mean?"

He lifted a bale of hay from the bed of the truck and walked unsteadily into a pen. He grunted as he dropped it into a container.

"It means it's never been my home. It's just a place to squat for a while." He spat and wiped his brow.

"Until when?"

"Until Aunt Grace gets sick of me."

"Jake, that's not true."

"No offense, Ms. Clark, but you don't know nothing."

The comment stung, taking her aback for a moment. Jake was hard. Harder than he was when he'd first arrived. Something had happened or was happening.

"You know you can talk to me," she said, hoping like hell he would.

"No use. It's not gonna help me when I got no place to stay."

"Jake, you'll always have a place to stay." He eyed her and she could see the forming tears. "Your aunt Grace—"

"No. Don't."

"And if not with her, then here."

He cut the strings off the hay and dispersed the numerous flakes to the other Rubbermaid containers.

His silence was killing her.

"Jake, what is going on?"

"Nothing, ma'am. Nothing new anyway. I'm just in the way. I'm a burden."

"That's not true."

He threw down the last flake of hay. "It is true! And you, you don't know nothing about it!"

He took off back into the stables and she hurried after him. She heard him crying before she saw him. He was balled up in a corner trembling with tears. His cap was at his feet and tears streaked through the dirt and sweat on his face.

She knelt next to him. "Tell me how it's true, Jake," she said softly. "Tell me."

"She—she—all she does is work. All the time. Even at night. She never even sleeps. She won't talk to me. She won't spend time with me. It's all about that fucking trial!" He began to sob again.

"I'm sure once this trial is over—"

"No. No." He shook his head. "There will be another one. And then another one. She's their go-to girl. She has to make partner. Whatever the hell that means. And me, well, I'm just in the way, aren't I? All she does is snap at me or ask me ridiculous questions. Ones I've already told her the answers to."

It was obvious Grace wasn't paying attention to him. But other things he'd said concerned her as well. She wanted so badly to ask him if Grace was all right, but she knew that'd set him off and he'd think she didn't care.

"Come on," she said, helping him up.

"Where we going?" He grabbed his ball cap and placed it on his head, wiping his tears with his wrist.

"It's lunchtime," she said.

"After that, can I ride out on the trail with you?"

"We'll see. But first I've got to make a phone call."

❖

Madison walked from the patio where the boys were eating to call Grace. She wanted her to answer on the first or second ring, but it went on to her voicemail.

"Grace, this is Madison. Can you give me a call back, please? I need to talk to you about something."

She ended the call and leaned against the house. What would she have said to her had she answered? *What the hell is going on? I'm worried about you? I'm worried about Jake?* None of it sounded like something Grace would want to hear, and it was already difficult enough just to get her to set foot on the ranch. Still…her worry got the better of her, and she looked in Jake's file and found the office number, and dialed.

"Grace Hollings's office," a female answered.

"Is Grace in?"

"No, I'm sorry. Grace is in court. Can I help you?"

"This is—Do you know when she'll be out?"

"I don't know. They are giving closing statements today, so it should be soon."

"Thank you."

"Are you sure I can't take a message?"

"Thanks, but no."

So Grace was in court. That's why she wasn't answering her phone.

"Damn." It would have to wait until afternoon. That is, if Grace didn't send someone else to get Jake. She hoped she wouldn't. She had some things she needed to get to the bottom of.

"Hey, Marv."

"Yeah?"

She pulled him aside from the patio. "I need to talk to Grace tonight."

"About what?"

"A lot of things."

"Why are you telling me?" he asked.

"Do you think you could take her over to the colt? When she first gets here?"

"Trying to soften her up?"

"I'm trying to keep her from leaving."

"What's going on, Maddy?"

"I don't know," she sighed.

"You really care about her, don't you?"

She paused and stared into the grass. "Yes."

He shook his head. "Well, I guess that's all that matters."

"Thanks."

"Don't thank me."

"Okay. I'll hug you instead."

"Oh, hell." He embraced her halfheartedly. "You know I think you're crazy, right?"

"Yes. I might be."

He laughed.

"I just know I can't stop worrying about her. That has to mean something."

"Yes, but does she feel the same about you?"

"I don't know." *I hope so.*

"Ms. Clark?" Michael was leaning on the patio rail.

"Yes?"

"Are we gonna saddle up the horses now?"

"I was thinking about it."

"Okay." He smiled.

"Go on over to Bobby and he'll get you started."

The boys all hollered with excitement as they scrambled for the barn. All of them except Jake. She scanned them twice to be sure. Then she went inside the house. His file was lying on the kitchen counter, open. She'd made sure she closed it.

"Shit. Jake? Jake?" she yelled for him up and down the hallway. "Jake, are you in here?"

He'd never wandered into the house alone before. He must've

been looking for her. And now he'd found the file. That couldn't make any kid feel good. Most of it was from the state's evaluation, and none of it was anything he would want to read.

"Jake?" *Please let him be in here. Even if he's holed up crying in the bathroom.*

But he wasn't in the house.

She trotted outside and found Marv. "You seen Jake?"

"No."

"Do you know if he ate?"

He shook his head. "Why?"

She ran to the stables where the boys were busy practicing how to saddle their horses on their own. They'd been taught the day before, and many had their horses all ready to go.

"Where's Jake?" she asked, starting to panic.

She got grumbles and shrugs.

"Did he eat lunch?"

The last time she saw him, he was pouring a glass of iced tea, waiting on the grilled burgers.

"He went in the house looking for you," Michael said.

"When?"

"A while ago. Before we ate."

"I saw him come over here," another boy said. "A while back."

"Oh, God." She hurried to Draco's stall. It was empty.

"Marv!" She pushed the crowding boys out of her way. Marv came sprinting from the house.

"What is it?"

"Jake's gone. And so is Draco."

He scanned the land around them quickly. "Where would he go?"

Her heart jumped in her chest. "He said something about the trail."

Marv raised an eyebrow. "Does he know which one?"

"No." There had to be a dozen out there, all leading out into the desert and over the mountains. No place for a child and a horse.

"Aw, shit."

"Bobby!"

Bobby came running from around the stables. "Is Jake gone?"

"Yes, why?"

He held up a note. Madison's heart sank as she read it: *I won't be back.*

CHAPTER TWENTY

Grace sped like a demon up the dirt trail and to the ranch. She slammed the car in park and flew out, running and collapsing in her heels.

"Where is he," she demanded. "Where's Jake?"

Marv helped her to her feet. "There, there. Calm down."

"Calm down? Don't ever say that to me again."

She moved past him to Madison, who was talking to a deputy sheriff.

"Where is he? Madison, where is he?"

Madison excused herself from the deputy and he crossed the lawn to regroup with the others. It was pushing on five o'clock, and it looked as though the other kids were gone. A helicopter loomed overhead.

"We don't know," Madison said. "He—the chopper has yet to see him, so we're thinking he's found some shade somewhere."

"Oh my God," Grace said. "I can't lose him. I can't lose him, Madison."

Madison pulled her in tight for an embrace, but she pounded her fists on her shoulders. "Where is he? Where is he!"

"Shh, we'll find him. We'll find him." Madison held her tight and felt her fragile body shaking beneath her arms.

"We're going to get a hold on his ankle bracelet, okay? We'll find him that way."

"Something's wrong," she said. "You should've already found

him, with a helicopter and the sheriff's department. He's a boy on a black horse, Madison. How hard can he be to find?"

Marv looked away and Madison pulled away from her. Her eyes were clouded with worry.

"Grace," she said. "We don't think he wants to be found."

"You think he's hiding?"

"Maybe."

"But why. Why would he do this?"

"We were hoping you might know. He left a note in Draco's stall. It said *I won't be back.*"

"Oh God. Oh God." Sobs overcame her. The world was closing in around her. Not Jake. Not Jake.

"Grace?" Madison helped her to the patio, where she eased her down in the shade. "You're bleeding," she said, touching her leg.

"I don't care." She jerked it away from her warm fingers. "All I care about is Jake. How could you let this happen? How?"

Madison shifted and folded her hands together. "I tried to call you today. Earlier, before any of this had happened."

"Why?"

"To find out what was going on with you and him."

"What do you mean?"

"Grace, he was really upset. And he said some things that worried me. Like how he was a burden to you and how your home wasn't his home. That he would soon have no place to stay."

Grace felt the tears come again. "He said that?"

"Yes. He said you don't talk to him and that all you do is work."

"He said he didn't have a home?"

"Yes."

She closed her eyes. "I shouldn't have told him. I just shouldn't have told him."

"Told him what?"

"That his mother left rehab. We—no one can find her."

"Oh, no."

"And that's not all." She hesitated, fighting tears. "Gabby left a note. It said *I won't be back.*"

Madison breathed in sharply.

"I shouldn't have told him."

"Well, he had a right to know."

"Yes, but now he thinks I don't want him. He thinks he has no home. He thinks I'm going to get rid of him." She laughed. "I actually thought he might worry about her coming to find him. Or I thought he might try to find her. Boy, was I wrong. Guess he knows her better than I do. She's long gone and she's not coming back."

"You can't be sure of that."

"Yes, I can. I am. We'll never see her again. Not after this time. She wants to disappear. She knows I have Jake, so now she's completely free. She's gone, Madison."

"Come on," Madison said, taking her hand. "Come inside."

"No. I can't. Not till we find Jake." She cried. "I love him so much and he doesn't know that, does he?"

Madison didn't speak, but she didn't release her hand either.

"It's all my fault. He started spending more time with you and I got jealous and I let work take over everything. He—he was trying to tell me this the whole time and I ignored him. I'm so awful." She collapsed into her hands, feeling like dying. If anything happened to him, she'd never forgive herself.

"You aren't awful," Madison said.

"No, please. I wasn't fishing there. I really have been behaving awfully. Oh God, if anything happens to him…Isn't there anything we can do? I feel so helpless just sitting here." She stood and tried to make her way to the deputies.

"They won't let us, Grace. They want us to stay here."

"I can't just sit here!"

"I'm sorry."

"Can't I take my car out and look?"

"They have men out there on horseback and SUV. Not to mention the chopper. They'll find him, Grace. I promise."

But Grace didn't want to hear it. She couldn't bear to hear it. They might find him, but would he be okay? Or would he have already hurt himself somehow? What if the horse had thrown him again?

She ran for the stables, feeling sick. She hadn't eaten all day. The trial had ended and they were waiting for the jury, but she honestly didn't care one way or the other. All she wanted was for Jake to return. And in the meantime, she couldn't bear to be out there doing nothing. She needed to feel closer to him.

The stable felt warm and smelled of hay and manure. She found her way to the first stall and opened the door. The colt was wary at first but then came to her when she knelt. As she inhaled his skin and felt his breath, she began to cry.

❖

"Grace, Grace." Marv was shaking her shoulder.

"Yes?" She bolted upright along with the colt.

"I've got good news." He smiled. "They found him."

"What!" She stood. "Is he okay?"

Marv nodded. "He's going to be fine."

She jumped in his arms and held him tight. "Oh, thank you. Thank you, thank you, thank you." Then she turned and kissed the colt. "Thank you, Colby."

"Colby?" Marv asked as she ran from the stall.

"That's his name," she called back. "He told me."

Grace tore off her shoes and sprinted out of the stables. "Where is he?" she asked the first man she saw. The man pointed to an SUV pulling up. Grace followed it as it slowed, and when the door opened, she yanked Jake by the arm and pulled him out and hugged him tightly.

"Oh my God. Oh my God," she cried into his ear. "Oh, honey. I'm so glad you're okay."

She couldn't let go of him. She wanted to hold him safe in her arms forever.

"I love you. I love you so much," she said, holding his face. "Do you hear me? I love you and I want you with me. I want us to have a home."

Jake's face twisted into tears. "I'm sorry, Aunt Grace. I'm so sorry."

She held him tighter and stroked his hair. "It's okay. It's okay now."

They held each other and cried even as the officer led them toward the ambulance. Grace shook as she continued to half hug him. He looked sunburned and dirty. His hair was mussed and coated in dried sweat and dirt. But he looked alive and strong. His eyes were bright and full of sorrow. She'd never seen him look so beautiful before.

"I love you, Jake," she said, laying her head on his shoulder.

"I love you too."

CHAPTER TWENTY-ONE

Madison watched from the patio as Grace and Jake were reunited. It was a beautiful sight to see, and she teared up herself at the love she could feel coming off them. As badly as she wanted to go to them, she knew they needed their space, and she'd done enough meddling to last a lifetime. Now it was up to Grace and Jake. She'd let him finish the program, but the rest was not her concern. She'd done her best to try, and that was all she had in her. As hard as it was to let Grace go, she had to. For all their sakes.

"Marv, let me know how Draco is," she said as she exited the patio.

"Where are you going?"

"Inside."

"You okay?"

"Yeah. Oh and let them know, Grace and Jake, they can stay here tonight if they want. I know that boy isn't going to want to go anywhere near a hospital."

"Okay," he sighed. "Will do." But before he walked away he stopped. "Oh, I found her in with that colt. They were curled up together. Never seen anything like it."

"Really."

"Yeah, and it was the darndest thing. She said he told her his name was Colby."

Madison smiled. "I'm not surprised."

"I have to admit I am. I've seen more heart in that woman tonight than I'd ever thought I'd see."

"I told you."

"I can see why you're in love with her."

"In love?" The words sort of smacked her.

He just smiled. "Don't bother arguing." He tilted his hat. "I'll go tell them to stay here tonight."

Madison settled back on the couch and tried to relax. But the day's events kept resurfacing, and she wondered if she really did need to change things on the ranch. Jake had managed to escape on a horse twice. Boys had done other things to cause trouble, but this one could have been life-threatening. She should've known better than to leave his side when he was so upset.

"Damn it." She rose and poured herself some iced tea, too strung up for wine. How had she messed up with two people she cared so much about?

"Hi."

Madison sank down on the couch as Grace entered the room.

"Hi," Madison replied.

Jake was behind her. "Ms. Clark," he said. "I'm so sorry." He started to cry again. "I didn't mean to cause so much trouble."

Grace hugged him and wiped his eyes. Madison stood and placed a hand on his shoulder. "I'm glad you're okay," she said.

"But you're upset."

"Well, yes, Jake. We talked about consequences. This is one of them. You took off again when I trusted you. You took my horse and you put both your lives in danger."

"Maybe now's not the time—" Grace said.

"Let her talk," Jake said. "I need to hear it."

Madison sighed. "I'm glad you're okay, Jake. Truly." She hugged him. "Your safety is my main concern."

"I didn't hurt Draco. He's fine. He rode real good."

"I'm glad." Madison rubbed her forehead. "How are you?"

"He's a little dehydrated but okay otherwise," Grace said. "I think more than anything he's just exhausted. And I am too."

Both did indeed look exhausted. She longed to tuck them into bed. "Well, you're free to stay here tonight."

"Are you sure?"

Madison nodded. "It's the least I can do. Besides, it's after dark."

"Thank you."

Madison showed them to the spare wing, where there were two bedrooms and a bathroom. Then she retrieved fresh clothes for them both.

"My room is down the hall to the left if you need me."

Grace smiled at her softly. "Thank you, Madison."

"Sure."

Madison left them to bathe and get ready for bed. Outside, everyone had left and she made her way to her own room to shower and get ready for bed. The day still swam in her mind and no answers were forthcoming. Sleep would not be easy, so she decided to turn on her record player and lie down with a glass of wine.

She chose Coltrane's "In a Sentimental Mood" and sat back onto her bed. The candlelight from her night table flickered across the ceiling. Lila and Flaca settled onto their beds and the night slowly eased in around her. She closed her eyes several times, sleep trying to come. The last time she opened them, Grace was at her door, and she had to blink to make sure she wasn't dreaming.

"Can I come in?" Grace asked.

Madison nodded.

"You weren't sleeping, were you?" She closed and locked the door behind her. She smiled as she took in the large room. "A fireplace in here too?"

"Yes."

"You're a romantic."

"Diehard romantic, I'm afraid."

"Wine?" she asked, coming to sit on the bed.

Madison couldn't take her eyes from her. She had on a long T-shirt and, it appeared, nothing else.

"Where are the pajama pants I gave you?"

She shrugged. "I was hot."

Madison grinned, knowing the wine had already reached her. "Yes, you are."

"Would you like to feel how hot?" Grace whispered.

"Yes."

Grace took her hand and kissed it delicately. "First I want to talk to you," she said and her eyes welled with tears.

"You look so tired, Grace," Madison said and touched her face. "So delicate and so tired."

"Shh, I want to say something to you."

"Okay."

"I'm sorry for how I've treated you."

Madison wasn't sure what to say. She didn't need her to apologize. She could see it all in her eyes and in her face.

"I've been a real bitch and I blew you off and I got jealous. I was just a mess. And then this whole thing with Gabby and the trial…"

"Grace, you don't have to explain."

"Yes, I do. And then today with Jake…something happened inside. Something huge. I realized that what I really needed and wanted was already in front of me. That I didn't need anything else."

"Jake."

Her eyes lit up. "Yes. And that I wasn't going to wait around for Gabby anymore. I don't need Gabby. I can raise Jake. As if he were my own. I want to. I love him that much." She shook her head. "My career, I need to make a change. I don't want or need to work that many hours. I just found out we won our case today and I don't even care. All I care about is Jake and…" She touched Madison's face. "You."

"Me?"

"Yes. God, I wanted to run to you, Madison. I've wanted to run to you for so long. I'm so sorry I pushed you away. I'm so sorry."

"It's okay. I—was ready to just let you go."

"That's not okay! Please don't let me go. I'm so ready for a change."

"Tomorrow's a new day."

"How about tonight?"

Madison smiled. "There is always tonight."

Grace bent her head and kissed her. "Mmm, you feel good."

"So do you."

"Do you want to feel how hot I am?"

"Oh, yes."

Grace took her hand and led it carefully up her thigh. But Madison drew back a little, kissing her deeper while stroking her skin lightly, up and down, tickling her leg.

"Oh, Madison," she said. "Mmm, hurry. Feel me. I'm already so hot for you."

Madison trailed her fingers up her thigh, lightly teasing with the back of her nails until she felt her bare flesh. Grace gripped her wrist and called out.

"Madison."

"You are hot, baby. So very hot. And wet."

"Mmm, yeah. I am. You do this to me."

"I do?"

"Yes. I almost couldn't wait to get out of the shower."

"Well, I'm glad you did."

"You do this to me all the time. Just with the look you give me. I see you wanting me and my body reacts at once." She started gyrating her hips and Madison found her so wet she easily slid her fingers up inside her.

"Oh God! Madison, yes."

"You feel so good," Madison said. "So, so good."

Grace gripped her shoulders and pulsed. Back and forth and back and forth. "Yes," she said. "Madison." She held her face and kissed her deeply, rocking on her.

"I love watching you like this," Madison said. "I think about it every second of every day. Your face, your body, the way you move, the way you feel."

"You d-do?" She quickened her pace.

"Oh, yes."

"Know what I-I think about?"

Madison grinned. "Tell me."

"I think about you and your hands. How strong they are, how they feel on me and in me. I used to…fantasize about your hands taking me, peeling off my panties and plunging inside me."

"You did?"

"Yes, and—and that's not all. I think about you in that little rugby outfit."

Madison laughed.

"I-I do. And I also think about you all sweaty and dirty in your jeans and T-shirt. How I'd love to just peel them off you in the stable one evening and go down on you right then and there."

"You would?"

"Mmm-hmm."

"Would you let me do that to you?"

"Oh yeah."

"Oh—God, this feels good."

Madison eased her onto her leg, careful to keep her fingers inside, and with her other hand found her clit with her thumb.

"Now," she said. "How's that?"

"Oh God!"

"Good?"

"Yes!"

Her body jerked and waved. Madison needed to see her. All of her. "Take off your shirt," she said. "Slowly."

Grace gave her a wicked smile and inched her shirt up oh so slowly, showing first her hips, then her etched abdomen and finally her taut breasts. She left it dangling around her neck.

"Pull on it," she said. "Pull on it and make me kiss you."

Madison, completely turned on by the demand, grunted and tugged on the shirt, pulling Grace forward for a fiery kiss.

"Now make me come," Grace said. "Make me come and hold me forever."

Madison kissed her, shoving with her tongue and with her fingers. She held her tight, holding the shirt firm with her fist while pumping her harder. And just when she thought Grace couldn't take any more, she plunged a third finger in, jerked Grace back, and sent her over while she rose and bit her neck.

"Madi—Madison—Madison!" she called out, head thrown back, neck sinking beneath Madison's teeth. "Oh God baby, oh God, I love you. I-I can't get enough of you. I…tried so hard to stop it."

And she collapsed on top of her, snuggling down into her arms. "I love you," she said and then broke into fresh tears.

"I love you, Madison Clark," she said one last time, looking into her eyes.

Madison touched her face, kissed her tears, and whispered, "I love you too."

CHAPTER TWENTY-TWO

Grace awoke at four thirty with the break of dawn. She was lying in Madison's arms, both women nude, candle long ago extinguished. She thought about waking her but something about the beauty of her sleeping changed her mind. Quietly and carefully, she kissed Madison's lips and slipped out of bed. She'd had the best night's sleep in weeks, and she felt so good she almost whistled on the way into Jake's room.

She found him fast asleep as expected, stomach down, one arm dangling off the bed. Beamer slept curled at his feet. She stroked Jake's forehead and then went to her room to slip on pajama pants and a pair of Madison's slippers. Then she walked the length of the house to the door and outside to the stables. The dawn felt fresh and crisp and the sprinklers were on, enveloping the lawn in a light mist. Lila followed at her feet as she made her way into the stables. As Grace entered and inhaled the scents, she imagined waking up like this every morning, in Madison's arms, walking out to a beautiful dawn, heading into the stables.

What a wonderful life it would be.

Madison had offered her that life last night. Just as she had offered herself, time and time again, allowing Grace to burrow between her muscular legs and make her cry out all night long.

It was a life she wanted and needed. But she had asked to take it slow and Madison had readily agreed, just wanting her to know she and Jake were welcome, any time.

"I'm so lucky," she said as she leaned on the stall door to watch Colby sleep.

"No way," Madison said, coming up behind her. "I am."

Grace laughed and enveloped her. "What are you doing up?"

"Me? It's four thirty."

"I know, I didn't want to wake you," Grace said.

"Your absence woke me."

"I'm sorry." But she wasn't really sorry. Her mere presence had just solidified the morning as one of the best ever.

"Don't be." Madison nibbled her neck and breathed deeply. "I found you."

"Mmm, yes, you did."

"So what are you doing out here?"

"Just came to see Colby."

"Colby, huh?"

"Yeah. That's his name."

"Is it, now?" Madison looked in on him and grinned. "He looks like a Colby."

"Told ya."

"How about you?" Madison asked. "What if I came out just to see you?"

"I'd say you definitely found me." God, how she could move her with just words.

"So how about I take you in that back stall and check you out?"

"I'd say that sounds real good."

"Really?"

"Oh, yeah."

Madison lifted her easily and carried her to the far empty stall where she placed her down gently, spread out a blanket on the hay, and lay down next to her.

"What do you want to check first?"

Madison laughed and lifted her shirt. "This needs to go," she said and then cupped her breasts. "So I can see these."

"Really? I thought you'd want to play with the shirt again." They'd used the shirt to bind and tug at each other all night. So much, in fact, it appeared loose and stretched and she was surprised they hadn't torn it.

Madison wasn't into the shirt, though. "I don't want it. I want these."

She took a breast in her mouth as she turned and pushed Grace back on the blanket. Grace struggled not to make noise and Madison tugged harder, slipping off her pants as she did so.

"Oh, Madison," Grace hissed. "Yes, baby."

"That's it," Madison said. "Make noise." She sucked her again. Harder and with more tongue in between.

"Oh! Mmm, fuck!" She arched into her and took Madison's hand and placed it between her legs. "I can't wait. I can't wait."

"My favorite spot," Madison said, bracing Grace's arms above her head. "Now I get to take you," she said.

Grace struggled playfully. "Yeah?"

"Oh yeah. First with my mouth and then with my hand."

"You're gonna have to hold me down," Grace said.

"I won't need to. Not for long." And she released her quickly, spread her legs with her powerful hands, and buried her face in her, licking at once from side to side and up and down with long movements of her tongue.

"Ah! Madison! Oh God!"

Grace gripped her head. The pleasure was so intense all she could do was hold on to her, even as her own body moved beneath her.

"Madison. Madison." She just kept saying it over and over as Madison groaned into her, licking and then sucking. The noise of it was as maddening as the pleasure, driving her insane, out of her skin, out of her mind.

"Come," Madison managed to say between long, tongue-pressured sucks. "Come in my mouth."

Grace tore at her head, the pleasure too great; it was building and building. Her body undulated, sweat lined her stomach, Madison's head moved against her, giving to her, giving her so much. Her clit was on fire with ecstasy, Madison's tongue bathing it and sucking it off, again and again. Until Grace was spreading herself further and jamming herself against her, trying to take her in. She grabbed at the hay, at the blanket, at all she could. But none of it was enough and none of it compared and as she grabbed Madison's head again she demanded, "More, more, Madison, more."

And then with Grace's heels in her back, Madison pressed harder with a strength Grace didn't know she had. And Grace came and shouted into the dawn and rocked her body against her, back arched and nipples hard and pointing at the ceiling. It was the most beautiful moment of her life and it hovered there, like a different dimension for what seemed like hours.

Madison between her legs with her hair disheveled with hay, the blue of the dawn against the rafters of the stable.

It all ebbed as her pleasure flowed.

Ebbed and flowed.

And as soon as it dissipated, she had to have more.

"Come here," Grace said, tugging her gently by the hair. She flipped her quickly and hurriedly removed Madison's shirt and slid her flannel pants down.

"Grace," she said, but Grace ignored her.

"Shh." Grace tore one leg of the pants off, spread her open, and dove into her wet flesh. Madison gripped her head and stifled a loud moan. Grace devoured her quickly, first saturating her clit and then holding it with her teeth as she flicked. It drove Madison crazy and she writhed beneath her, saying incoherent things.

"Grace. Grace. Love. Oh, Grace. Lo-ve this. I…want you. Want you o-on my face."

Until finally she sat up and came, abs tight, shoulder muscles etched, neck strained, voice caved.

"Yes, Madison. Yes!" Grace said as she continued to get her off, using her tongue to swirl on and round her clit.

But Grace hadn't had enough. She needed more. More of a connection. "I want to fuck you," she said. "While you fuck me."

Madison was breathless and collapsed onto the blanket. "Yes," she said. "Okay."

Grace gently slid in at once and found her unbelievably tight. "Oh my."

Madison sat up a little, her entire body tight. She groaned and eagerly went inside Grace.

"Yes," Grace cried. "Madison, this is so beautiful."

"Yes," Madison breathed. "You are so beautiful."

"We are," Grace said.

"Yes."

"This is," she said.

"Yes."

"I love you."

"I love you," Madison said.

"Fuck me."

They pumped each other, filled each other, and tugged at each other. Until both were sweating, pulsing and gasping at the in-and-out motion.

"More?" Madison asked as their climaxes mounted.

Grace nodded, looking down on her beautiful face and incredibly strong body. She could smell her scent and her cologne, mixed with the hay. God, she wanted to tear at the earth to get to her. Just claw at her in the dirt and hay, never able to get enough.

Grace eased in another finger and Madison did the same, causing Grace to scream in ecstasy and come all over her hand.

"Yes, baby! Madison, yes!" Her body moved on its own and she focused on Madison's face as long as she could, both of them coming apart together, Madison clenching her fingers tightly, holding her inside.

"Grace!"

"Madison, I love you," she finally gasped and collapsed atop her. She breathed deeply and quickly, inhaling the hay through the blanket. She laughed, all throaty and spent. "I love you so much."

Madison bit her neck and flipped her, looking down into her eyes. "And I love you."

She went further down and lightly kissed her thighs. "I want to give you more," she said, looking up at her with her burning hazel eyes. She licked her way inward and whispered, just before Grace could protest, "Gently."

CHAPTER TWENTY-THREE

The day was salted with sun, most of it filtering through sporadic clouds, high in the sky. Madison eased back on her elbows and smiled, loving watching the boys as they tossed the rugby ball around and shouted.

The trail ride was a big success so far, and the grill smelled magnificent with Marv and Bobby at the helm, flipping burgers and hot dogs. A breeze came through and blew the paper tablecloths and swished through the horses' tails and manes. It also blew through Grace's blond hair, and Madison found herself captivated by her once again, this time taking the long, pleasurable moment to stare at her wholeheartedly.

As if feeling her eyes, Grace turned and caught her with a smile.

"Hi," she said coming to lounge next to her on the thick blanket. The desert hummed and bloomed around them, jackrabbits and lizards scurrying, Beamer and Flaca chasing.

"Hi, yourself."

Grace slipped off her designer shades and gave her a quick wink. "This is some shindig, Ms. Clark."

"Think so?"

"Heck yeah. I'm lovin' it."

"Think the others are?"

"I think so. Everyone's laughing and smiling. The horse ride was a big thrill. I know for sure my ass will hurt from here to eternity."

Madison laughed. "I have a remedy for that."

"I hope so. Because we haven't even ridden home yet and I'm sore."

"Everyone will be. Even the boys."

Grace stared out at them, looking thoughtful. "You know, Judge Newsom called and told me what you did."

"Oh?"

"She said you pleaded with her not to put Jake in juvie for his latest escapade."

"I don't think he belongs there."

"Where does he belong?"

"With you. And here, at the ranch."

"Are you sure?"

"Yes." She shifted and crossed her feet. "He needs more therapy, though. More than he gets here."

"I agree."

"The judge agrees too."

"Thank you," Grace said, touching her hand. "Really."

"Don't thank me. Jake did this. If he hadn't worked so hard and changed so much, I would've let him go. But I believe in him."

"You don't know how much that means."

"Yes, I do. Just like I know how much it means that you didn't give up on him either."

Grace wiped a tear and replaced her glasses. "You're a damn good woman, Madison Clark."

"Don't say that yet. You haven't seen his chore list."

Grace laughed. "Oh, no."

"Yeah, he isn't going to be thrilled."

"Actually, I think he will be. I know he's very grateful to you for all you've done for him."

"Oh?"

"Yes. And I've been meaning to tell you…he came up with quite the story the other day. Told me he set the whole amusement park thing up so we would get together."

"Get out of here."

"He did. He also said he's been wanting us to be together for a long while."

"He has?"

"He's very insightful. Said he tried every trick in the book," Grace said, laughing.

"Ha."

"And that we were too dumb to see it."

"Well, we were dumb," Madison said with a grin.

"Yes."

Madison tipped her hat and looked at her. "Does this mean you two will stay for dinner tonight?"

Grace smiled. "Are you kidding? Jake wants to stay the night. He even brought May's horror movies to watch."

"Really?"

"Yes, so break out the wine, I'm going to need it." She leaned in close. "And later let's play that Coltrane song again."

Madison licked her lips. "Okay."

"So I can love you all night long."

"And I you," Madison said.

"This time well past dawn."

"Yes."

"Wholeheartedly."

About the Author

Ronica Black is an award-winning author and a three-time Lambda Literary Award finalist. Her books range from romance and erotica to mystery and intrigue, and she enjoys trying her hand at all. Ronica also enjoys drawing, painting, and sculpting. She lives in Glendale, Arizona, with her partner, where she relishes a rich family life and raising a menagerie of pets.

Books Available From Bold Strokes Books

Wholehearted by Ronica Black. When therapist Madison Clark and attorney Grace Hollings are forced together to help Grace's troubled nephew at Madison's healing ranch, worlds and hearts collide. (978-1-60282-594-9)

Haunting Whispers by VK Powell. Detective Rae Butler faces two challenges: a serial attacker who targets attractive women, and Audrey Everhart, a compelling woman who knows too much about the case and offers too little—professionally and personally. (978-1-60282-593-2)

Fugitives of Love by Lisa Girolami. Artist Sinclair Grady has an unspeakable secret, but the only chance she has for love with gallery owner Brenna Wright is to reveal the secret and face the potentially devastating consequences. (978-1-60282-595-6)

Derrick Steele: Private Dick—The Case of the Hollywood Hustlers by Zavo. Derrick Steele, a hard-drinking, lusty private detective, is being framed for the murder of a hustler in downtown Los Angeles. When his brother's friend Daniel McAllister joins the investigation, their growing attraction might prove to be more explosive than the case. (978-1-60282-596-3)

Nice Butt: Gay Anal Eroticism edited by Shane Allison. From toys to teasing, spanking to sporting, some of the best gay erotic scribes celebrate the hottest and most creative in new erotica. (978-1-60282-635-9)

Initiation by Desire by MJ Williamz. Jaded Sue and innocent Tulley find forbidden love and passion within the inhibiting confines of a sorority house filled with nosy sisters. (978-1-60282-590-1)

Toughskins by William Masswa. John and Bret are two twenty-something athletes who find that love can begin in the most unlikely of places, including a "mom-and-pop shop" wrestling league. (978-1-60282-591-8)

me@you.com by KE Payne. Is it possible to fall in love with someone you've never met? Imogen Summers thinks so because it's happened to her. (978-1-60282-592-5)

Worth the Risk by Karis Walsh. Investment analyst Jamie Callahan and Grand Prix show jumper Kaitlyn Brown are willing to risk it all in their careers—can they face a greater challenge and take a chance on love? (978-1-60282-587-1)

Bloody Claws by Winter Pennington. In the midst of aiding the police, Preternatural Private Investigator Kassandra Lyall finally finds herself at serious odds with Sheila Morris, the local werewolf pack's Alpha female, when Sheila abuses someone Kassandra has sworn to protect. (978-1-60282-588-8)

Awake Unto Me by Kathleen Knowles. In turn of the century San Francisco, two young women fight for love in a world where women are often invisible and passion is the privilege of the powerful. (978-1-60282-589-5)

Franky Gets Real by Mel Bossa. A four-day getaway. Five childhood friends. Five shattering confessions…and a forgotten love unearthed. (978-1-60282-585-7)

Riding the Rails: Locomotive Lust and Carnal Cabooses, edited by Jerry Wheeler. Some of the hottest writers of gay erotica spin tales of *Riding the Rails*. (978-1-60282-586-4)

Rescue Me by Julie Cannon. Tyler Logan reluctantly agrees to pose as the girlfriend of her in-the-closet gay BFF at his company's annual retreat, but she didn't count on falling for Kristin, the boss's wife. (978-1-60282-582-6)

Snowbound by Cari Hunter. *"The policewoman got shot and she's bleeding everywhere. Get someone here in one hour or I'm going to put her out of her misery."* It's an ultimatum that will forever change the lives of police officer Sam Lucas and Dr. Kate Myles. (978-1-60282-581-9)

High Impact by Kim Baldwin. Thrill seeker Emery Lawson and Adventure Outfitter Pasha Dunn learn you can never truly appreciate what's important and what you're capable of until faced with a sudden and stark reminder of your own mortality. (978-1-60282-580-2)

Murder in the Irish Channel by Greg Herren. Chanse MacLeod investigates the disappearance of a female activist fighting the Archdiocese of New Orleans and a powerful real estate syndicate. (978-1-60282-584-0)

Sheltering Dunes by Radclyffe. The seventh in the award-winning Provincetown Tales. The pasts, presents, and futures of three women collide in a single moment that will alter all their lives forever. (978-1-60282-573-4)

Holy Rollers by Rob Byrnes. Partners in life and crime Grant Lambert and Chase LaMarca assemble a team of gay and lesbian criminals to steal millions from a right-wing mega-church, but the gang's plans are complicated by an "ex-gay" conference, the FBI, and a corrupt reverend with his own plans for the cash. (978-1-60282-578-9)

History's Passion: Stories of Sex Before Stonewall, edited by Richard Labonté. Four acclaimed erotic authors re-imagine the past…Welcome to the hidden queer history of men loving men not so very long—and centuries—ago. (978-1-60282-576-5)

Lucky Loser by Yolanda Wallace. Top tennis pros Sinjin Smythe and Laure Fortescue reach Wimbledon desperate to claim tennis's crown jewel, but will their feelings for each other get in the way? (978-1-60282-575-8)

Mystery of The Tempest: A Fisher Key Adventure by Sam Cameron. Twin brothers Denny and Steven Anderson love helping people and fighting crime alongside their sheriff dad on sun-drenched Fisher Key, Florida, but Denny doesn't dare tell anyone he's gay, and Steven has secrets of his own to keep. (978-1-60282-579-6)

Detours by Jeffrey Ricker. Joel Patterson is heading to Maine for his mother's funeral, and his high school friend Lincoln has invited himself along on the ride—and into Joel's bed—but when the ghost of Joel's mother joins the trip, the route is likely to be anything but straight. (978-1-60282-577-2)